Two men. One a royal born and bred, the other…not.

Prince James lives a life of stifling duty behind the walls of Buckingham Palace. He keeps his secrets and his stiff upper lip while dreaming of the day he will be free to find the man of his dreams. It's a day he believes might never come. Until Prestidigitation Jones, an ethnobotany student from a small town in Australia, bursts into his life.

Prestidigitation marches to his own beat along with his small group of family and friends. He long ago accepted most people found him a little eccentric, but that won't stop him from living on his own terms. Though happy enough, Presti dreams of finding a man who accepts him as he is and loves him unconditionally.

A fated meeting throws them together. An attraction blooms, and a friendship begins. Distance keeps them apart, but destiny brings them together.

Through a trail of exposed secrets, false starts and unfathomable tragedy, James and Presti's feelings for each other grow stronger. Does James have the courage to fight for his dream? Can Presti face the public scrutiny of being the plus one of the spare to the throne?

Surely together, they can find their way to happiness/find their happily ever after.

DEAR PRESTI:

THE PRINCE'S

PEN PAL

KARRIE ROMAN

A NineStar Press Publication

www.ninestarpress.com

Dear Presti: The Prince's Pen Pal

First Edition, December 2024

ISBN: 978-1-64890-830-9

Also available in eBook, ISBN: 978-1-64890-829-3

CONTENT WARNING:

This book contains depictions of the death of a secondary character and grief.

For Astrid, Per Ardua Ad Astra.

Chapter One

SOME PEOPLE HAVE a unique gift bestowed on them at birth. Perhaps one they enjoy bragging about or showing off at parties, performing these oddities like show ponies. The only gift I possessed seemed to be attracting unwanted attention.

Unlike many in these strange days of reality TV and phone cameras, I preferred to remain unnoticed. Anonymous. Out of the spotlight. Thank you very much. My dearest friend, Astrid, delighted in pointing out how I drew attention as if I were a magnet. She blamed the fantastical way I'd entered the world. She claimed that it was simply not possible for me to remain in the background after I'd burst onto the world stage in such a public way at my unusual birth.

I adored my best friend even if she did have an annoying tendency to be correct.

Though I attempted to move wraith-like through my days, I

tended to stand out like a rainbow on a grey day. That's how my mother described me, at any rate.

I did not like this state of affairs one little bit.

On this overcast day, the rainbow hovered just out of sight as I attempted to wade through the press of bodies on the overcrowded bus. I tried to move silently, ghost-like. Moving this way and that, shifting to avoid others so I didn't so much as graze anybody.

"I beg your pardon. Did you say you're studying poo, young man?" The woman screeched as I pressed against her legs. She clacked her knitting needles at a prodigious rate of knots, quite heedless of how perilously close they were to poking the large man sitting next to her.

"No, ma'am. I said I'm trying to get through." All eyes were fixed on our interaction, except those who chose sensibly to travel on public transport using earbuds. Those people remained happily serenaded by Bruce Springsteen or some other artist. Eminently sensible, I thought.

The octogenarian knitter nodded and returned to her stitches, leaving me to smile awkwardly at those around us.

Mentioning poo is not the best place to start my story — and I swear there will be no further scatological mentions — but I must begin this tale somewhere.

Much like life, when we are thrust kicking and screaming into this world, starting at the beginning is the best way to go. So it is at my birth that we must begin.

My fantastical birth, as previously hinted at, is quite the tale. It's also where some might argue I peaked as a person and had my promised fifteen minutes of fame, all in one ignominious day.

All this greatness and celebrity happened to me the day I was born, so I don't remember it myself, yet I feel pretty scarred by it, nonetheless. For better or worse, I also own plenty of photos and articles to look back on so I can reminisce about my extraordinary birth. It's not everyone who can claim a naked photo of themselves on just about every worldwide newspaper front page.

You see, my mother, the sweetest and kindest woman I've ever known, is also somewhat odd. At least my grandfather always described her as such. I prefer to think of her as one of those people that extraordinary things happen to. I think it was from her that I received my gift.

Her strict, conservative father, Grandpa Joe, never had any flavour to his life that I ever saw — no joy. He fancied himself the keeper of everyone's soul. He lived miserably while trying to save us all from hellfire and brimstone. To my young eyes, he seemed melancholy. He may have loved stomping about his run-down home — asylum, as I liked to think of it — swearing at the television as if the people he cursed might take the trouble to answer. He apparently never found any happiness in it though. A smile from Grandpa Joe would be like stumbling across a blooming corpse flower.

When I think back on Grandpa Joe, sadness at his misery most often strikes me. More times than I could count, I tried to tell him not to worry about what everybody else was getting up to or with whom and instead enjoy what he had around him. Nine times out of ten, he bit my head off for my trouble. The one time out of ten he spread his arms wide and asked, "Enjoy what exactly?"

Poor Grandpa Joe, whether he loved the curmudgeon life or

not, it loved him. Mum liked to say that being such a cranky old fart kept Joe alive until his early eighties when he rightfully should have died much sooner. Grandpa Joe loved his daily whiskies and packs of smokes. A courageous doctor once told him that he had the heart of a ninety-year-old. Of course, Joe was only sixty-eight at the time. But that was Joe.

He wasn't often proud of Mum and me, but he shone with pride the day I was born, or so I've been told.

Getting back to that day, you should know that our queen—bless her—has been on the throne for sixty years this year. But when I was born, it had only been forty glorious years. Her fortieth year of reigning coincided with Australia hosting the Olympic Games. It was a festive year for Australia. Our highest medal tally at the games and our longest reigning monarch all in the same three hundred sixty-five days. Celebrations spilled onto the streets.

That year was a big one for my mum too. First and most importantly—she always says—she got pregnant with me. Around the same time, she successfully applied to be a volunteer at the Games. It was to be her first job, not that she'd be getting paid, but just the same, Grandpa Joe proudly told everyone he met. Mum had never had a job before. Too flighty, Joe had often said. Her head always in the clouds. Mine would have been, too, if I'd had to listen to Grandpa ranting and raving daily.

Anyway, Mum volunteered at the Olympic Games and did quite a good job. People liked her good heart and kindness. Grandpa Joe seemed to be the only one who cared about her flightiness and general lack of ambition. In fact, Mum made the news a few times during the games for being Australia's best mascot, showing the world the kind of people we were.

Mum became so well known that when the queen went on a Commonwealth tour as part of her ruby jubilee — rubilee as Mum called it — she insisted that my mum and a handful of other volunteers were present at the athletes' meet and greet. Imagine Grandpa Joe's face when he discovered his daughter would meet the queen. Well, we don't know what his face was because he'd kicked Mum out for getting pregnant without a husband by then. I guess it's self-explanatory that he took her back, but that wasn't till after I was born.

So, the athletes' parade happened, and we all ended up at Government House for luncheon with the queen. I say we because, of course, I was there in my mum's belly — but there just the same. During the luncheon, each athlete and volunteer was presented to the queen with cameras rolling for the poor folk at home to gander at.

The volunteers were to be presented at the end, but Mum told me later she didn't care; she'd have waited all day to meet Queen Anne. Mum admires the guts out of that older woman. Even to this day, she'll stand and sing "God Save the Queen" as loud as she can whenever she hears it, no matter where or when. No matter that it hasn't been our national anthem for decades.

I guess that explains why Mum didn't let the little fact that she'd been having labour pains all day deter her from her chance to meet Her Majesty.

The doctors told Mum later that I must have been crowning when Mum attempted an ill-advised curtsey before the queen. Rather appropriate term, I always thought — and so too did the newspapers when they reported on the baby who'd been born at the feet of the monarch. "Couldn't Wait to Meet His Queen," one newspaper headline had declared. That same article described how I'd shot out of my mum and landed on the royal toes. Mum never liked that article. She hated how common they had made it sound, talking about Her Majesty attempting to catch me like a football punt.

And so, there was my fifteen minutes of fame. Photos of my newly-arrived-into-the-world, utterly naked body lying at the feet of Queen Anne splashed in the worldwide media. A few also showed pictures of the queen's stunned expression or my mother's contorted face as she pushed the last of me out.

Queen Anne bore the hubbub well. She'd looked down at me and then at my mother before saying, "Well, that is either the best bit of prestidigitation I've ever seen, or you've just had a baby, my dear."

And that was how I got my name.

Prestidigitation Jones.

Though I go by Pres or usually Presti. My poor mum didn't know it was a word meaning conjuring tricks when she decided on it for my name. She'd thought the queen had been naming me at the time, and she wasn't going against the queen's wishes.

Mum and I were a bit of a hit for a while. Media wanted to speak to us, and even my dad stuck his head into things — for a while, anyway. Gambling and women lured him right back once our fame declined. I'm glad about that, really. From what I've heard, he was not the kind of dad I would want around.

All this occurred twenty years ago, and a lot has happened in the meantime. Grandpa Joe died. Mum eventually got a paying job. I went to school and made a friend like young people do, but as yet, I'd not done much to surpass my inimitable birth. And I was happy about that.

But our past had caught up with us. Mum and I received an invite to the palace as part of Queen Anne's sixtieth year on the throne celebrations. A reunion, if you like. We could each bring one guest to one of several diamond jubilee dinners planned over the year. Mum's still working on shortening that one. Dibilee was the current frontrunner, but it didn't have quite the same ring as rubilee.

Mum will be taking Howard. They've been together six years now, and though he is not my dad, he treated me like his son. Better…he considered me a son he both loved and liked. But best of all, he treated my mum as if *she* were the queen.

I will be taking my best friend, Astrid Rhys-Bomalier. She's also my only friend. Though she has a boyfriend who told me that any friend of Astrid's is a friend of his, so I have him as a friend now. Astrid is so good at being my friend that I don't miss having others. Grandpa Joe used to say people steered clear of me because they found me hard work and somewhat of a *fruit loop*. I knew he was right, but I didn't actually care. I liked my life, and I liked who I was. I didn't see why I needed to change any of that to please other people.

I was on my way to Astrid's now. Since I invited her to meet the queen, she's had a near constant bout of nervous dyspepsia. She often told me she had no idea how to act or what to wear. I would try again to get her not to worry. In her sixty years of ruling, I expect the queen had met just about every kind of person we could think of. A nineteen-year-old-vegetarian-glow-worm enthusiast who only wears shades of blues and purples wouldn't be too shocking for her. Of course, as Astrid's boyfriend unhelpfully reminded us, purple is the royal colour, so it may be unseemly to don such a shade before Her Majesty. Protocol can be so fiddly.

Astrid lives in a sex shop. Not in it, precisely, but above it. In one of those very out-of-date units they used to build over shopfronts, presumably for the shop owners to live in. Not that Astrid owns the sex shop or even works in it. She only shares the back gate with F*ckingham Phallus.

This brings me to one of those coincidences in life that can't help but make me smile. Astrid has lived above F*ckingham Phallus with her father for years. Indeed, before she ever met me. Of course, once she did meet me, we laughed for hours over the fact I'd once been naked in the royal presence while Astrid lived above a shop given what could only be the porn name of the queen's home. We both felt it must be fate bringing us together.

Glorious.

Managing to deboard the bus far more easily than I'd boarded, I strolled down Maxim St with my gaze down. I knew this street as well as the freckles on the backs of my hands. This town had always been my home. Small and insignificant, I considered it the grandest place on earth.

Peter, Paul, and Fairy's Bakery was on my left. Fruit Tingles on my right, its doors overflowing with fresh produce. Dominic's Domesticated Menagerie loomed halfway up the block. I wouldn't say I liked walking past that place. If one must keep an animal, the least one could do was rescue one of the multitudes at the shelters. I often asked Dominic to get at least some of his animals from the shelters. He refused, once telling me he didn't want any 'mangy, rejected has-beens 'in his store. That was the day I first met Constable Dickens.

You can imagine Dominic's surprise when Constable Dickens told him he'd uncovered no evidence of me striking Dominic even though Dominic's speech was muffled due to his bleeding nose. After Constable Dickens listened quite patiently to Dominic's retelling of the story, he didn't even ask me if I'd done it, nor did he show interest in my split knuckles. He just sent me on my way with a warning to avoid the shop in future. I guess it helped that I was barely twelve at the time.

To be clear, I don't make a habit of physically assaulting people whose ethical moralities do not align with mine. But I'll admit I lost control when I heard him use abhorrent language to describe the adorable little mites from the shelter.

"Hey, Presti. Going up to see Astrid?" Silkie Bellbird popped her head out of the shop's back door as soon as I neared the stairs leading up to Astrid's. I had no doubt she'd watched me arrive on the security cameras inside the shop. Her massive eyelashes almost dusted the tip of her nose as she winked at me.

"I am. And you've gone red again." Silkie's hair, always voluminous, now flamed the brightest red I'd ever seen.

"You know what they say about redheads, dahling."

I shook my head. "Um. No."

"We're red on the head and fire in bed." Silkie winked again and cackled.

I loved Silkie. Kind and sweet, she'd always been good to Astrid and her dad. The first time I'd met her, she'd been without her wig and had scared the bejesus out of me with her deep, booming voice and often maniacal laughter. Silkie has owned

F*ckingham Phallus since the '70s. She'd called it a far more discrete name back then—and claimed many times that she never planned to retire or sell. With her applied-with-a-brickies-trowel make-up and glitzy costumes, Silkie described herself as a relic of the early days of drag queens. Every time I looked at her, I could see decades of a life well lived in her sparkling eyes.

"Oh, sweet boy, I just love making you smile. Made use of your gift yet?" Silkie asked, that hint of mischief glistening in her eyes.

Just the mention of the present Silkie gifted me for my twentieth birthday ignited fire beneath my skin, flushing crimson across my cheeks. "You could have warned me you'd already put batteries in it," I muttered.

Silkie pouted her full lips and tipped her head quizzically. Sighing and rolling my eyes, I continued, "It went off in my backpack during a pop quiz in class. When Mr Jamison made me pull it out to stop disturbing the class, it literally jumped out of my hand and across the floor like a prostate-massaging energizer bunny."

Silkie threw back her head and cackled again. "My god, sweet boy, this is why I love you. Do not ever change."

Still laughing, Silkie slunk back into her shop, flaming bouffant red hair and all. I couldn't bear to tell her Mr Jamison had kept my new and—thankfully—unused prostate massager. He'd had it for over a week, and I never wanted it back.

Astrid waited for me at the top of the stairs. She would have laughed with me about the prostate massager in gentler times, but these were not those times. In exactly two days, we were leaving for London, and Astrid still needed an outfit for meeting the queen.

"Where the hell have you been, Presti? No, do not answer; I know where you've been. Downstairs confabulating with Silkie." Astrid's dewy, wide green eyes locked on mine. She could be a little high-strung, my best friend. I adored every bit of her. One of the things I love best is her extensive vocabulary of many unusual words. Sometimes it made keeping up with her complex, but never boring.

Astrid's father, Paul Bomalier, is somewhat of a recluse, rarely setting foot outside his front door. Fortunately, he works from home, and Astrid is old enough now to run out for anything he might need. Paul loves books. Specifically, books on words and the English language. Hence Astrid's extensive and unique vocabulary. Naturally, some of that has rubbed off on me, which my mum thinks is splendid. She's often said that I might have dropped from the queen's loins rather than hers with the way I speak so posh sometimes.

"I only just got here, Astrid. And I'm early. You said four, and it is now three forty-two."

"Semantics," she answered, waving her hand in the air. "I have seven frocks to try on. I've got quite the collywobbles about the whole thing. Plus, poor Larry is quite beside himself. He says he simply cannot choose because I will look positively radiant in all of them."

Larry — Lawrence Brooke-Brooks — adored Astrid almost as much as I did. They'd been a couple for a little over four months, but it would have been longer if Larry had managed to ask Astrid out before then. He'd spent the first two months after meeting her fumbling his words. He would flush a colour something like beetroot and run, quite flummoxed, from her presence. His awk-wardness had been adorable to watch at the beginning. But wit-nessing his discomfort became quite excruciating after a while.

"Well, we best get in there and rescue him," I said as I stepped through the door she held open for me.

Larry Brooke-Brooks sat in the centre of the emerald-green sofa. His long legs spread wide, his gaze transfixed on Astrid. They were a handsome couple. Both were tall and long-limbed, but Larry's sharp masculine features were a lovely contrast to Astrid's round face, wide eyes, and full lips — something of a che-rubic angel to Larry's more equine appearance.

"Hello, Larry," I greeted, dropping my backpack to the sin-gle armchair adjacent to the sofa. No sign of Paul Bomalier yet.

"Afternoon, Presti. How's things?"

"Quite good. They'll be a sight better once we've got poor old Astrid's frock sorted out." I flopped onto the end of the sofa. Larry squirmed and shifted to accommodate my presence, yet managed to do so without unlocking his gaze from Astrid.

"I'll try the first one," Astrid said as she strode from the room, leaving Larry and me alone.

"Listen here, Presti," Larry began as soon as Astrid's bed-room door shut with a snick. "You will take care of her in Lon-don."

He wasn't so much asking me as telling me. An order not to allow any harm to his beloved. Not that he needed to remind me. I'd never let anything happen to Astrid. "Of course. I won't let her out of my sight."

Larry finally looked over at me, his dark eyes watching me quizzically. "Never understand how you're not madly in love with her. Glad you aren't, mind, but…"

"I love Astrid, Larry. I'm just not *in* love with her." We'd had this conversation often, especially after Larry had been into Paul Bomalier's batch of Mai Tai. One terribly awkward time, Larry burst into tears because he just couldn't believe I could be so close to Astrid and not fall terribly in love with her.

Silly. But Astrid thought it was the sweetest thing ever.

Larry shook his head and mumbled, "Never understand it." He hadn't found the courage to ask me about my sexuality yet, though I could see the words on the tip of his tongue.

Before either of us managed to utter another word, Astrid burst into the living room, wearing the first gown up for consideration.

She looked appalling.

Like a giant purple feather duster, trussed up in a somewhat hideously bedazzled, feather-adorned monstrosity. I searched for the right words while Larry gushed and enthused beside me. Much of Astrid's inner strength resembled steel, but a misplaced, thoughtless word could quite easily hurt her.

"Well, Presti?" Astrid asked after a time.

"I should think we'd want to look a little less…showgirl and a little more…Astrid."

Astrid looked down at herself, nodded and smiled. "Quite right, Presti. Not me at all."

With that, she flounced—as one must in a dress such as that—back into her room and shut the door. The following four dresses were much the same. Not that they were all as ostentatious and gaudy as the first, but none of them were Astrid.

The sixth dress fit her like a glove; the rich purple

illuminated Astrid's green eyes. A hint of glamour with very little glitz. Not a trace of bedazzlement in sight. Understated, classy, and beautiful. Like Astrid.

Larry looked like he might need paramedics when Astrid stepped out in the deep violet number. His eyes almost popped out of his head like a cartoon character, his words spluttering from him. "Perfect," he choked. "Just perfect." I'm pretty sure I could hear his heart thundering in his chest despite the two-foot gap between us.

"He's right, Astrid." I smiled as she twirled in the gown. Though aware there'd be more royalty at the shindig than I presently knew existed, I could not envisage any of them outshining Astrid.

"It is rather stunning. Not a popinjay in sight with this one." Astrid's smile lit up the small room. At that moment, I understood why Larry wondered at anybody who wasn't in love with Astrid. Her whole heart and soul made up her smile.

"Not a popinjay at all."

"Right." Astrid put her hands on her stomach and gazed down at herself again. "This is the one, then." She fled to her room, and though I knew there was another dress we hadn't seen, I also knew we never would. Astrid knew her own mind and, decision made, she never looked back.

Though Astrid offered, I didn't stay for dinner. I'd have her all to myself in two days, and I knew Larry needed to store up as much Astrid time as he could. I'd expected him to join us on the trip, but work commitments would keep him here. None of us ever spoke of the ill-thought-out two days he and Astrid had kept apart in the early days of their relationship when neither had wanted to be *those* people. The ones who couldn't bear to be apart from their paramour, but somehow that was exactly what they were.

The mournful message Astrid left on my phone on the first of those two days remains saved in my message bank. In case I should ever need to blackmail her.

As I left, Larry pulled me in for our first-ever hug. He manfully slapped me on the back and whispered for me to take care of his heart for him. It took me entirely too long to realise he meant Astrid. By then, she'd overheard and weepingly declared herself the luckiest woman alive to have such a love. Time for me to make myself scarce.

By the time I finally extricated myself and slipped out the door, they were—rather violently, I thought—embracing and pledging they'd never be apart again upon Astrid's return.

With only fifteen minutes until Mum finished work, I thought I'd head over to join her for the walk home. We had a car, but Mum drove like a toddler in a dodgem car, and I wouldn't say I liked operating anything with wheels. I had scores of unopened toy cars from my childhood as proof.

I've never been so happy as when Mum transferred to the local branch of Fosters' Pawn Stars because it was walking distance from home.

Calling it a local branch sounds rather like Fosters was a giant chain store. Peter Foster had two pawn shops, but he had his eye on a location for a third. Pawning was big business these days, and Peter could see his fortune rolling in.

Mrs Bucket—who surprises everyone she meets by not insisting it's pronounced Bouquet like the lady on the telly—wrote a harshly worded letter to the local paper about the downfall of our suburb when Fosters moved in. First F*ckingham Phallus and now Pawn Stars, she'd bemoaned; soon, we'd be known as the sex capital of Australia. She still gives Mum the stink-eye whenever they cross paths, though she is always nice enough to me.

"Hey, Mum." I waved as I approached the counter, the bell tinkling, chasing me into the store.

"There's my boy." Mum beamed at me. "How did it go with Astrid?"

"She's picked a dress. We have a twenty-hour flight and an entire day in London before the party to practice behaving with royalty. So, I thought I'd leave her to spend time with Larry." I rounded the counter and pecked my mum on the cheek. She sometimes gets a bit teary when I hug or kiss her. Most of her friends 'sons stopped doing that when they were pre-pubescent, apparently.

"Wonderful. Howard's picking up the suits today; my dress is almost ready. Not long now." Mum smiled wide. This would be our first trip overseas—our first time in a plane too—and we could not wait. We'd never have managed it except the queen had paid for our tickets. Not the queen exactly, but some way through her. We only had to pay for accommodation and spending money.

"Do I get to see your dress before? Or will it be a surprise?"

"Definitely a surprise."

I have an entire photo album filled with images of me in my mother's creations. She is an excellent seamstress; it's the design aspect she struggles a little with. I like to think that wearing the clothes she made for me taught me resilience. By the time I was twelve, I never gave a damn anymore what the other kids thought of my outfits. It was either stop caring or spend afternoons balled up and rocking in the corner.

As far as I was concerned, it was time I got to spend with Mum while she designed and created clothes for me. I'd spent hours and hours sitting with her by the machine, both of us prattling on about this or that while she worked. Sometimes I'd read aloud while she sewed. I wouldn't trade those memories for all the peer popularity in the world.

It didn't mean I wasn't just a little concerned about what she might wear to meet the queen. But in the end, so long as it wasn't crotchless chaps teamed with some nipple-exposing top, I'd be just fine.

"Well," Mum sighed, reaching for her handbag. "That's it. Finishing time. Let's go home, Presti."

We walked through the main street, cut across the bowling club, and made it home just as the sun began to set with its gorgeous pinks and purples on the horizon. I may well have peaked on the day I was born, but my life was nothing to complain about.

Chapter Two

JAMES, YOUR GRANDMOTHER wants to see you," my father said the moment he stepped into the room. No matter that I hadn't seen him in a week, he didn't even offer a 'hello, how are you? I missed you terribly' first.

My older brother and several younger cousins simultaneously cried, "Ooh, James is in trouble." In terrible sing-song voices to boot, because they were arseholes.

"Hello, Dad. Good to see you. Missed you terribly," I replied to a unanimous response of stunned silence. We weren't *that* family. We didn't joke around; we weren't playful.

Sighing, I shuffled from the room, straightening my tie as I went. No matter how hard I tried, I couldn't pinpoint the exact moment my life began teetering on unbearable. If anybody knew I felt that way, they'd no doubt call me a spoiled sod, and they'd have a point. It just didn't seem fair that there'd been a social movement encouraging people — indeed flat-out ordering them in many cases — to live their authentic lives. Be who you are. Don't let anybody tell you how to live or that you're somehow wrong for being you. Those were the cries to arms these days.

From where I stood, it applied to everybody but me — and my family, to be fair. But they all seemed quite happy with who they were and how their lives were progressing. What did we have to complain about? We lived in an actual palace and were waited on hand and foot. We had everything a person could need, but we didn't have freedom.

"James, dear. Come in, come in," Gran greeted me as I entered her office.

Smiling, I took the armchair across from Gran while trying to avoid the piercing glare of Simon de Montfort — no relation, as he likes to remind people — as if everybody knows about the thirteenth-century nobleman who led a revolt against a tosser king but turned out to be an even bigger tosser himself.

"Good afternoon, James," Simon said once I'd settled into my chair.

"Simon." I nodded, quickly returning my attention to Gran. "Everything okay, Gran?"

"Yes, dear. Yes, of course. I wanted to revise the plans for Saturday with you." Gran glanced up at me briefly as she spoke, but her gaze returned to the notes in her lap. Splendidly spry for eighty-one, Gran knew more about upcoming engagements than anybody else in the family. Perhaps Simon could give her a run for her money, but he'd be the only one.

"I'm to sit at table three," I replied, searching my mind for the plans we'd gone over just yesterday. Come Saturday, I had no doubt my lifetime of training would kick in, and I'd know exactly where to sit and to whom to talk.

"Right, quite right," Gran muttered, her attention increasingly held by whatever fascinating titbits were in those notes. As usual, she could hardly give a moment of time for her second oldest grandson and spare to the throne no less.

"Your table," Simon broke in, "consists of several people Her Majesty has met over the years who became quite popular with the media and the people at the time. There is no one of great importance at the table, but having them there should make for some good press coverage."

Simon might be no relation to *that* de Montfort, but he was a complete tosser just the same. I sometimes wondered if he even realised that we were, in fact, in the twenty-first century, and royalty wasn't quite what it was back in the heyday. We couldn't walk around randomly beheading our subjects anymore. An increasing number of citizens would be happy to turf us out of our palaces on our posh arses.

"I suspect those people are of great importance to someone." Especially given that one was a previously popular Prime Minister of the United Kingdom. Not even that appeared to warrant a label of importance in Simon's mind.

Simon eyed me coldly, his mouth twisted and ready should this turn into another one of my frequent reminders to him that we are no better than anybody else simply because of the family we'd been born into. Most of my family were relatively caring and did good work for charities, but on this point, I stood alone. They definitely thought themselves top of the social ladder.

"Well, of course, James, dear," Gran intervened with her

uncanny ability to know precisely when to step in to calm the choppy waters. "Simon simply means there are no heads of state at your table, no current ones anyway." Gran smiled, and I smiled back.

She was the queen, but she was also my gran, and I loved her. "You know I didn't mean what happened last month, Gran."

Gran eyed me speculatively over the rim of her glasses. I'd been hauled over the coals by my father and palace courtiers over the unfortunate incident with the Russian president, but Gran had smiled, patted my hand and told me she doubted we'd be going to war over it. "I know, James. I think President Petrov would be much happier if he could learn to laugh at himself just a little. And Chef really should have explained that you did not need to toss the chocolate bomb quite so hard."

Photos of President Petrov with his face covered in custard and edible glitter splashed across the papers the next day, with some wondering if I'd purposely hurled dessert at a foreign leader as a statement against the treatment of Russian citizens by his increasingly totalitarian regime.

Gran did her best to stifle a grin while Simon glowered at me. "In fairness," I added, "Mrs Musa from Nigeria wound up with strawberries in her hair, and she was seated at George's table."

Simon cleared his throat because he was a dick and hated anybody exceeding the time he'd allotted them to spend with the queen. "Yes. Well, the point is, James, that I have sent you an email detailing the guests at your table with photographs attached and a brief history. I certainly hope you'll use this so that you can converse with these people."

First of all, I wanted to say but knew it'd be a waste of time, he should be addressing me by my title, which he does for every other member of my family. And secondly, I'd been conversing with people from all walks of life, including world leaders, since I was a toddler. Talking to people wasn't my problem, at least if it wasn't a large group.

On the other hand, talking to them as just James rather than His Royal Highness, Prince James Henry Philip George, the spare of the heir, was a massive problem. I didn't know who *just James* was.

"Simon?" Gran said in her voice that four hundred years ago would have meant heads were about to roll. "Could you give James and me a moment, please?"

Always indefatigably polite, Gran also knew that Simon, of all people, would never argue with her. He rose stiffly, clearly not accustomed to being dismissed and certainly not for my benefit. He nodded, shot me a glare and backed out of the room as if waiting to be recalled after discovering being kicked out had been an enormous misunderstanding.

As soon as the door closed behind him, Gran said, "James, are you quite all right?"

There was no doubt in my mind that it had not been her intention to make me feel guilty, but I did, nonetheless. Here was an eighty-one-year-old woman who'd been on the throne for sixty years. Sixty years filled with public service and putting everything before her needs or wants. And here I was at twenty-one, already complaining about having to give so much of myself to a role I didn't choose or—and this was the crux of the matter—want.

"I'm splendid, Gran," I tried, knowing from her tilted head and *oh, come on* expression that she did not believe me in the slightest. "It's just…well, crowds and the like… They're not actually my thing." I went with my trusted excuse for not relishing my role. I'd had coaching to help me feel more at home speaking to an audience. Nobody understood, though, that this was not the life I wanted for myself.

My fault really because I hadn't said a word about it to anyone.

Gran nodded, stood, teetered for a moment as many older people, I expect, do, and then came to sit in the chair at my side. She reached for my hand, gently threading our fingers together before pressing a kiss to the back of my hand. "I know you do not enjoy being the centre of attention, James, and public speaking gives you quite the horrors, but the more you do it, the easier it becomes."

I nodded. I knew she was right, and I had to get used to it… But what if I wanted to be a doctor, drive a bus, or be cabin crew for British Airways? Why did everyone else get to choose their life but not me? "It's a good thing George came first, really," I said. "It wouldn't do for the king to flush beet red and stumble over his words when all eyes were upon him."

"Perhaps we should consider a few more engagements for you, dear. Get stuck into it, as it were. Fake it till you make it, I believe they say." Gran smiled, but it didn't reach her eyes. I wondered how she truly felt, right down deep, about essentially forcing her grandchild into doing something he really did not enjoy.

"Maybe, Gran." I kissed the back of her hand and stood. "I better get reading about my dinner companions before Simon has a fit."

"Good boy." Gran patted my hand before releasing me. By the time I reached the door and turned back to smile at her, the queen was back in her seat, focusing intently once more on the pile of notes on her lap.

Deciding to avoid my brother and cousins, I went directly to my room, booted up the computer, and opened Simon's email.

Saturday's event was really a relatively small affair: twelve tables, each with ten people apiece. Most consisted of one or two members of my extended family and eight or nine visitors, who were either relevant now or had made an impression on Gran over the years.

I'd be alone at my table, given I had no partner to speak of. I browsed the names of those sharing my table — Colin and Regina Bishop with their three children, Braxton, Miles and Giselle. I knew the family reasonably well.

Regina had been Prime Minister for twelve years when I was a schoolboy, and for a time, she'd been more popular than Gran. Then there'd been a terrible scandal. Photographs had appeared, taken by a very long lens through a very small gap in their curtains, showing Regina and Colin with a cucumber being used somewhat unseemly. The beginning of the end of poor Regina's career began that day. On the other hand, Colin's career seemed to take off after the publication of the photos.

We had a long way still to go as a society.

The remaining four people were Howard Leigh, Penelope Jones, Prestidigitation Jones and Astrid Rhys-Bomalier. I reread the third name several times, but it always came back as Prestidigitation. Who in the hell named their child that?

Intrigued, I read the short bio which Simon had provided about him. Aged twenty, his claim to fame and reason for attendance had been that he'd had the blind luck, or perhaps misfortune, to have been born in front of Gran at a reception for thousands, including Olympic athletes, their families, and the media.

Simon had attached a photo.

Lying on the ground, umbilical cord still attached, and covered in things I didn't care to think too intently on, was a newborn baby. His face scrunched in his first howl of displeasure at being thus dumped into the world. A set of feet, similarly covered in whatever goo I was still determinedly ignoring, rested nearby. I wouldn't go so far as to say I recognised the feet, but I did recall hearing this story many years ago, so I knew them to be Gran's feet. No photograph of an adult Prestidigitation had been supplied.

As I read the other biographies, I discovered that Prestidigitation was to be accompanied by his mother, her boyfriend and his friend Astrid. They were flying in from Australia. Actually, they'd be in the air right now. They resided in some place called Kincumber. Which I really thought had to be a bad joke, given they would be seated with the Bishops and the spectre of their cucumber fiasco.

A quick internet search presented Kincumber as quite a small little locale to the north of Sydney in an area described as the Central Coast. There were other wonderfully named neighbouring places, such as Woy Woy and the rather delightful, Watanobbi. I'd always found those Australians to be quite an unusual lot. Forever shortening words. Case in point, an Australian lad I went to school with insisted he call me Jimmy because James was too much of a mouthful. No matter how often I pointed out the two names had the exact same number of letters, he wouldn't have it. He was a kind chap, though, so I'd let him—and only him—call me Jimmy, occasionally Jim.

Back to Prestidigitation and Co. His mother, Penelope, worked at a pawnbroker called Fosters 'Pawn Stars. That alone had to have been sufficient to give Simon de Montfort palpitations. I wondered how hard he'd tried to get the Kincumberians uninvited.

Howard, as an optometrist, might have raised their perceived respectability, but I believe—in Simon's eyes—the group would have sunk again when he discovered Prestidigitation worked part-time as a paper towel sniffer—whatever the hell that involved—to put himself through his studies in a science degree majoring in ethnobotany. Swinging the pendulum back to more social acceptability, Astrid was studying animal psychology.

At the very least, they seemed an interesting bunch. I wondered how they'd get on with the stiflingly boring—with the exception of the cucumber incident—Bishops.

A knock on my door dragged my attention from the Australians as George entered without waiting for me to invite him in. "How'd it go, old boy?" he asked, sounding more and more like our father every day.

"Fine. They just wanted to go over Saturday's arrangements with me."

George looked… Well, he looked like a perfect blend between our father and mother: mother's colouring and large, deep blue eyes, father's sharp features and broad shoulders. I, on the other hand, didn't. Gran often says she can see our ancestors in me, but to be honest, I'm somewhat surprised nobody from the media has suggested I'm a changeling or the result of an affair. I look about as much like I'm related to the rest of my family as I do to the Imperial Family of China — if they still had one, that is.

"Are you certain you don't want Cordy to come along as your plus one?" George rather nervously asked. We'd had versions of this conversation many times.

"Quite certain. It's not fair to her, George. I'm not interested in her like that, and the more the press sees her with me, the greater the speculation over when an announcement will be made." The perfectly lovely Cordelia Southwark, the twenty-year-old daughter of the Earl of Derby, had been my date at a handful of engagements. She had top-notch manners, regularly socialised with the elite of society and had a lovely, elfin appearance. She held no interest for me other than as a friend.

"You know Mother and Father are pushing for you to find someone to at least date for a lengthy period. Tabloids are already speculating that you must be a womaniser because you've never had the same lady on your arm for more than two engagements at a time." His tone suggested George was practising his I-am-the-king tone that he hopefully — at least I thought so — wouldn't need to use for a considerable time yet.

"I'm twenty-one, George. I don't want to settle down —"

"Yes, but you aren't even playing the field, James. There hasn't been a single shot of you stumbling from a nightclub with your face pressed into some unsuitable girl's barely concealed cleavage."

"Isn't that a good thing?"

"It's a bloody unusual thing, James." George pinched the

bridge of his nose as if I was exasperating him. He'd be decidedly less vexed if he kept his nose out of my life as I did for him. "There's already talk—"

"Of what?" How could there be talk when I did precisely nothing to talk about?

"That there's something wrong. That you aren't…well, normal. Most young men are at least dating a woman, sometimes many, but you…"

"I've dated," I said defensively.

"Attending a pop-up artistic display entitled 'Saucepans ' with one of the artists does not count."

This conversation, as all I have with my brother, would do nothing but circle and circle until we were both angry, frustrated, and had completely forgotten what we'd initially begun speaking about.

Tonight, I was too tired. "Look, George. It really is too late to add someone to the invite list at this stage, but I promise I will endeavour to get a date for the jubilee day parade. Deal?"

George looked me up and down with that glimmer of disapproval so familiar to me. "Deal."

Apparently satisfied with our talk, George left.

People may well call me a spoiled sod for being increasingly disgruntled with my life, but they weren't the ones walking in my shoes.

Chapter Three

OH, PRESTI. WHAT is that saying? Kansas has fled the building?"
Astrid's grip on my arm tightened as we walked in a processional
into a grand ballroom or perhaps dining hall. Architectural terminology of palaces was not my strong suit.

"I'm not certain that's quite right, Astrid, but I get your
meaning."

Not even Misty Cavanaugh's wedding to Olga Rimini came
close to matching the splendour of this event—and that had been
the social event of the decade. At least it was according to Pat
Malone of the *Kincumber Khronicle*. It was the first legal lesbian
wedding in the district after the referendum. I lost count of how
many times Misty had come crying to Mum, crumbling under the
pressure of the well-publicized event. It had been made clear to
her that anything but a well-turned-out reception in the Ettalong
Diggers function room would have been a catastrophe.

Misty would need to spritz the lavender and magnolia calming mist she'd become quite addicted to during her wedding preparations in quite enormous quantities if she were here now.

Several round tables dotted the room. Each held a subtle yet ornate floral arrangement surrounded by perfectly set place settings. Fine, delicately patterned dinnerware waited only to be filled with whatever delicacies were on the menu. Light flickered off the shining cutlery that must be worth double the value of Mum's small home.

Place cards decorated with richly calligraphed names of the guests adorned each setting. Hues of yellows, oranges, beiges in the flowers, and napery gave the enormous space a sense of warmth.

"Well, I must say, I am somewhat disappointed," Mum muttered behind me.

Try as I might, I could not imagine what about this spectacle disappointed her. "Perhaps the jet lag has got to you, Mum. What on earth is lacking here?"

"It is not the jet lag, Presti. I expected candles at the tables is all."

Ever the peacemaker, Howard added, "Perhaps, Penelope, we should be grateful for the lack of candles. I should think we've seen quite enough of candles after the incident at the Robinson's Joshua-finally-passed-his-driver's-exam-on-his-thirty-fourth-attempt party."

"Yes. Quite so, How. Of course, I still maintain that one should not invite one's guest to twirl in their newly created frock without at least warning them of the possibility of knocking over the numerous candles spread about the place." Mum answered in a manner that was not…her. Come to think of it, Howard spoke with a bit more…poshness than usual. A plum in their mouths, I believe, is the term.

"Why are we all talking like the queen?" I asked.

"When in Rome, dear," Mum answered. "Besides, you talk like this all the time, Pres. We can't have you showing us up." She smiled and winked.

At last, one of the butlers—footmen? Again, the correct terminology escaped me; at any rate, a finely attired gentleman—gathered us from the procession and led us toward our table.

Thus far, we'd only briefly sighted the royals, each resplendent in royal attire. Though nowhere near as expensive and elegant as theirs, I thought our little group looked entirely satisfactory in our finery. Howard and I wore the tuxedos we'd hired at Erina Fair. They fit…mostly well. I would have liked a little extra length in the legs, but I believe showing your socks is something of a fashion now. Astrid, naturally, looked stunning in her frock, and my mum… Well, the dress she'd made was remarkable. Entirely sewn from hand, I don't think someone fashionable could have looked better. She'd chosen an off-white fabric and festooned it with sparkling diamantes across the shoulders and at the top of a short tail beginning at the small of her back.

Looking at Mum and Astrid in their magical frocks, I found it difficult to believe any of this was real.

At our table, we were to be hosted by Prince James, royal wild child or recluse, depending on the day of the week or which magazine you picked up.

As a rule, I did not follow the tabloids. Actually, the only means I used to keep myself up to date with the news of the world — or at least my tiny section of it — was the *Kincumber Khron-icle*. Tabloids, though, I steered clear of and did not understand on any level.

Firstly, why were we all so terribly interested in what other people were doing, celebrities or otherwise? Secondly, I suspected that the people who worked for these rags sat around a table each week and decided which fantastical lie they'd spread about said celebrities in the following week's edition. It seemed to be a competition for the most bizarre tale they could create.

I'd often sat in Howard's waiting room, flicking through months- or years-old magazines with claims splashed all over the cover. Claims that, over time, turned out to be utterly false nonsense. Pregnancies, marriages, divorces. Speculation on the lives of celebrities meant only to sell copies of their peddled trash magazines.

Along with practising our formalities, Astrid and I spent much of our flight reading as much as we could about Prince James. All while doing our best to politely dislodge the sleeping gentleman who shared our row from our shoulders. We'd taken turns in the window seat as much for the view — not that there was much of one at thirty-something thousand feet — as for a reprieve from the slumbering gent who possessed no sense of physical boundaries.

He had, though, on one of the few times he was alert, regaled us with the time he'd met the hairstylist responsible for the locks of the queen's stable hand's aunt. It was a pretty momentous moment in the fellow's life and, by virtue of sharing his experience, ours. I suspected he might be one of the palace insiders the tabloids relied upon for their *news* on the royals.

"Oh, my gods, Presti. There he is," Astrid squeaked as we neared our table. "He's quite immaculate, isn't he?"

That's not quite the compliment Astrid thinks it is, given that she tends to judge others on the immaculateness of their bathrooms. But the prince was...well, gorgeous, frankly.

He wore a tuxedo, as did most of the men present, yet his fit crisply and perfectly accentuated his broad shoulders and trim waist. I tried not to tug at my ill-fitting rental enviously. Prince James's hair, an interesting mix of caramel waves interspersed with flecks of copper, fell in that purposely careless way just a fraction too long to be acceptable at the Tuggerah Lakes Secondary College.

From this distance, I still couldn't decide if his eyes were blue or green, but intelligence lurked behind them as he watched our approach. An intelligence that never seemed to be attributed to the prince, according to the research Astrid and I had done. I suppose being an intelligent, thoughtful young man didn't sell quite as well as being caught chugging a pitcher of beer, shirtless, barefooted and with your fly half open in a back alley behind a nightclub notorious for backroom sex parties.

As we neared, Prince James favoured us with a glorious smile. And I don't think I'm embellishing when I say it looked like the sun coming out: warm, bright, and startlingly beautiful. His eyes held on to the intelligence I'd spotted across the room, but now there was an entirely unexpected hint of shyness or vulnerability thrown into the mix. His eyes were, in fact, a blend of green and blue, leaning towards a teal colour.

Not to put too fine a point on it, but the presence of Prince James devastated me in a way I had never experienced, as if the solid ground I'd always stood on had suddenly dropped away.

"Good evening," he said, holding his hand first to Astrid, who shook it politely and silently.

Then it was my turn. I took the prince's offered hand, dropped into an ungainly combination of bow and curtsey and — staggeringly — kissed the back of his hand. As if not entirely done with making a fool of myself, I then proceeded to thank *him* for coming.

For a moment, he said nothing. Then, squinting adorably and looking at me as if not quite believing I was real, he stammered, "Well, yes. Of course. You are quite welcome."

Determined to keep up the pretence that I was, in fact, the host and he the guest, I turned to introduce my mother. "This is my mother, Penelope, and her partner Howard. Mum, this is Prince James," I said, entirely unnecessarily.

Mum glared at me. "Yes. Thank you, Presti." Quickly shifting to an apologetic smile, she turned to the prince. "It's a pleasure to make your acquaintance, Your Majesty — shit, no. Your Highness. Only the monarch is 'your majesty'. Damn it, I knew that. And I've gone and cursed in your presence."

"Is she for the tower, then?" Howard asked, at the same time offering his hand for a shake.

"Smooth," Astrid whispered. I shot her a glare, but once again, she'd nailed the situation.

"Not at all." Prince James laughed. "I am so delighted you all managed to make it such a long distance to be here for Gran tonight. I know she is thrilled. She's never forgotten your first meeting."

"Well," Mum said, "I did ruin her pair of perfectly grand

shoes."

Polite laughter ensued, and I did my best to fit back in after my earlier gaffs. A glance at the table warned me I'd be sitting on the prince's left for the evening. A thought that left me shifting nervously and trying to wrangle the butterflies fluttering a riot in my stomach. A pool of warmth spreading low in my belly that I'd never experienced accompanied the nerves. Could I be sick? I sent a silent prayer to whomever it may concern that I wouldn't end the night ruining another royal's footwear with bodily fluids that should not be shared.

The prince and I both reached for Astrid's chair, awkwardly chuckling as we pulled it out for her. Astrid looked between us and murmured, "Um…"

Poor Astrid could not take her seat with us standing on either side of it. In tandem, we stepped away, leaving Astrid the choice of turning her back on either me or the prince. She smiled at him, glared at me and sat, swiftly pulling her own chair in before we had the chance.

By unspoken unanimous assent, we let Howard seat Mum and took our seats.

"Hello," Mum said to the five other guests at our table — people already seated and watching our arrival with some amusement. "You must be the Bishops…es? Or is it Bishops?"

"Yes. The Bishops," Mrs Bishop replied. "I'm Regina. Colin. Braxton, Miles, and Giselle." She pointed to each member of her brood as she named them.

Regina Bishop and Mum exchanged polite conversation while we settled in, unfolded our napkins on our laps and the like. I was acutely aware of Prince James at my right elbow. Giselle

Bishop, whom I took to be somewhere about our age, sat on his other side. They were murmuring together.

"Okay, Presti?" Astrid whispered.

"I made something of a fool of myself," I muttered.

"It wasn't so bad—"

"I kissed his hand and thanked him for coming, As."

"You did, rather." Astrid held my gaze for a moment before we both snorted a laugh, drawing the table's attention. Thus far, all the practice we'd done on how to behave in royal company appeared to be a resounding waste of time.

"So," the prince's voice snapped me back to the present. "Prestidigitation, I believe you…um…work with paper towel?"

My ears flushed red and hot. As a general rule, I didn't give a tiny rat's behind what people thought of me. I'd long ago learned most thought me somewhat of a nuisance or not worth bothering with. I'd made my peace with that. My family and friends—ever expanding with the arrival of Larry—were all I needed. I liked who I was and did not intend to change for any-body.

But I'd never met anybody quite like Prince James before. Here was a man who lived in palaces, jetted about the globe at-tending all manner of soirees and functions, played polo profi-ciently and looked like he belonged with the gods of beauty and perfection. I couldn't help but feel a tad self-conscious about my job, temporary though it may be.

"Please call me Presti, and um, yes. Yes, I do," I tried with as much bravado as I could muster. I suppose I should be flattered he'd gone to the trouble of learning about me, but did he need to learn quite so much?" I sniff it, you see."

Prince James laughed and said, "I'm afraid I don't. Why do you sniff it?"

"The concise answer is to ensure it remains odourless. Paper towel should have no scent at any stage in its lifespan. Thus, it's my job to, in effect, judge that it does so. Remain scentless, that is." Prince James stared at me with the same look I'd seen many times before when people were puzzling me out. "Not the most glamourous of vocations, but it pays well. Certainly enough to keep me during my studies."

"Ah, yes. Ethnobotany, I believe. I must admit I had to look it up."

I nodded sagely. "Mm. Most people do. It really is quite fascinating. Australia's Indigenous culture is a marvel when it comes to plant use. Food, medicine, tools, and weapons. A marvellous and unique relationship with the botanical environment. We — and by we, I mean humanity — have lost so much of that relationship with nature. Apparently, humanity isn't quite as brilliant as we like to think we are."

Prince James's lips curled into a grin I couldn't quite read. Not the beaming smile from earlier, something more like amusement. He wouldn't be the first to laugh at my expense.

"I agree," he said. Mocking or not, I couldn't tell. "We have quite forgotten how to live co-dependently with the natural world. We're too busy taking advantage of it instead."

Prince James took a small sip of the wine that magically appeared in his glass — and mine, for that matter. I hadn't even noticed the waiter. I followed the prince's lead, wetting my dry mouth. Nerves continued to bubble in my gut, yet Prince James had an ease about him that was beginning to settle those bubbles.

"I believe you, too, are committed to working with nature, Astrid?"

There wasn't a question so much as the prince allowing Astrid to speak about herself. She ran with the opening. "Indeed. Animal psychology is my great enthusiasm—such wonderment in the animal kingdom. So much we don't yet understand. And to think some people think animals to be quite vacuous. Absolute balderdash, though I'd expect nothing less from most bipeds."

While Astrid diverted the prince with her pronouncements on the intelligence of the non-human species, I took a moment to regroup. Despite a few hiccups, I thought the evening might not be going too shabbily at all. Of course, it was early days, but it could have been so much worse.

Prince James interacted with Astrid with interest, whether politeness or not. How many dinners like this had he sat through? How many people had he had to be interested in when he'd likely rather have his eyes pecked out by a raven? He may be fabulously wealthy and deliciously gorgeous, but I didn't envy Prince James at all.

"And I believe you work in a pawnbrokers, Ms Jones?"

I returned to the conversation when the prince turned to my mother. Despite never feeling ashamed for what my mother did for a living before, I blurted out, "Yes. She assists with those who wish to pignorate."

The whole room seemed to quiet and still at my declaration, though I knew it wasn't the case. Astrid had found the term for pawning something in one of her father's books months ago, and we'd all—Mum included—laughed ourselves silly over it. Nobody laughed now.

"It…um. It means to pawn something. Pignorate. And, of course, pignoratitious refers to the pawned item," I explained, shame at myself flaming my cheeks. "Quite a funny word." Finally, I stopped talking.

"My dad," Astrid began, attempting to save me, "collects books about words, especially unusual or no longer used. Presti and I… We learn them."

"How…unique," one of the Bishop children muttered.

Nobody else at the table spoke, but they all leaned closer. Were they waiting for some other blunder to slip from my lips? They would not be disappointed. I could feel Astrid vibrating at my side. I couldn't look at Mum. "King Charles the Sixth of France sometimes thought he was made of glass," I blurted into the stifling silence. "He used to wrap himself in blankets to prevent his buttocks from shattering. We like to…learn strange facts also."

Fortunately, at that moment, a gong of some kind sounded. From the movement around the room's edges, I took that to mean dinner was served. Prince James — finally able to drag his stunned gaze from my person — turned to say something to Giselle on his right.

"Are you okay, Presti?" Astrid whispered.

"Did I just say the word 'buttocks' in front of royalty?"

"Afraid so. You only spout general knowledge facts or ramble when you're terribly nervous. It hasn't happened for some time."

Astrid was right. Social events didn't make me nervous. Of course, I was invited to so few that I couldn't be sure if that was true or if I'd just been lucky so far. Visits to the doctor, flying — I'd recently discovered — giraffes and needing to operate anything with wheels made me nervous.

"I knew that," Prince James said. His voice was so near that I jumped a little. He'd moved so close; his thigh pressed along mine with a startling zap. I expected him to jerk away from the touch, but he didn't.

"Pardon?" I managed.

"About King Charles. Thinking he was made of glass. Glass delusion, it's called. Quite popular amongst royalty and nobles, actually." The prince leaned closer, his lips near enough that his breath stirred my hair. "Thankfully, it doesn't seem to run in my family." And then he winked.

"I wonder why it was popular amongst royals and nobles?" I mused aloud, fascinated by the prince's revelation and doing my best not to quiver after the prince's wink.

Prince James shrugged in a manner quite un-regal but adorable, nonetheless. "Perhaps it was a way of expressing how exposed and fragile they felt in their public lives."

I stared at the prince whose gaze was far-off, somewhere over my shoulder. It sounded very much as if he spoke from experience. Not that I believed he had this glass delusion. But I could easily believe he felt that fragility and vulnerability. How could he not when he lived in a virtual glass bowl, the whole world watching each moment of his life?

Our first course was presented: some kind of soup. Green soup. I wouldn't call myself a fussy eater; more discerning, I'd say. As I sat there staring into my green soup that looked for all the world like something from Shrek's swamp, I berated myself for not considering the menu in more depth.

"Oh," Mum exclaimed, "pea soup. How delightful." She

smiled around the table before her gaze came to rest on me. Part of my discerning taste is to eat only things I know the name of. I mouthed a thank you and a return smile before tucking into my food.

The meal went rather well, given the few hiccups at the start of the night. Conversation flowed; we all managed to eat without spraying food across the table or snorting wine out of our noses. Prince James conversed with the Bishops as much as my little group, though he knew them well. Mum and Regina Bishop appeared to get on like old friends. All in all, I'd say our little table amid all this grandeur did quite well.

And Prince James kept his leg pressed to mine the entire time.

"We'll move into the music room now," Prince James said as waiters removed our dessert plates like magic. "There'll be tea and coffee, and we'll be free to move around to chat to…well, everyone present."

"Thank you, Your Highness," I replied. We'd received a briefing on the evening, but I thought it kind of the prince to ensure I knew what would happen. He must know how very out of place my family and I felt here.

"Please call me James," he replied with a soft smile, a rather delightful dimple forming on his left cheek. He'd asked me to call him James earlier in the evening, but I, somehow, hadn't thought of him as just James quite yet. He'd been warm and kind all evening, but he was royalty. I don't know what I expected of royalty. Aloofness, cold condescension, but Prince James—James—didn't fit that image at all.

As I continued to stare, apparently beyond fascinated with

that charming dimple, Prince James shuffled under my gaze. "Is there something the matter?" he asked, his fingers gliding across his face. Undoubtedly, he was searching for traces of food he might have left behind.

"Not at all," I replied. "I just noticed your dimples. Dimples are actually a deformity. S-something about muscle not f-forming correctly," I stammered, painfully aware I'd just insulted a prince of England. It seemed I was pretty determined to get myself thrown in the Tower.

James roared with laughter. Loud enough for guests at neighbouring tables to turn our way. "Now, that I didn't know," he bellowed, not even trying to curb his amusement.

Astrid poked me, rather viciously I thought, in the ribs. "Oh Presti, do try not to insult our host," she whispered, though her tone strained with unreleased laughter.

We didn't leave the stateroom in the same procession as we'd entered it, but there did seem to be a hierarchy of sorts as we exited. From the briefing, I knew that we would be introduced to the queen as we entered the music room.

In my head, I mumbled through the words I would speak and rehearsed an imaginary bow as we approached. James strode ahead of me, looking as wonderful from behind as from the front. I needed to stop thinking about how beautiful he was, especially as the queen — his grandmother — stood about two feet away.

Diminutive and silver-haired, she was anything but frail. She exuded a presence that would draw the eye even if she stood here in a sarong and a pair of thongs rather than the glittering jewels and evening gown. If I had to describe Her Majesty in a single word, it would be…formidable.

"Gran," Prince James murmured as he bowed slightly before kissing her cheek. "This is Prestidigitation Jones."

I took a step nearer, bowed low, and shook her hand. "Your Majesty. Thank you for having us this evening."

"A pleasure, young man. You've grown since I last saw you."

The three of us laughed politely, and then I was whisked away in the momentum of the receiving line. Astrid, Mum, and Howard all traversed their introduction to the queen with no fuss or fiascos. Then we found ourselves in a sea of people, most of whom we did not know.

Mum pointed out a few other royals and one or two minor celebrities. Otherwise, the room, like the evening, had been filled mostly with ordinary people the queen had encountered through-out the many years of her reign. I supposed, for whatever reason, these had stuck in her mind.

"Look at this room!" Astrid exclaimed. "I feel like I'm in a fairy tale."

"I thought that happened when you met Larry," I replied, twirling my gaze about the room like Astrid's. Mum and Howard had gone to join the line for tea, leaving Astrid and me to wonder at our surroundings. Not long after we'd met the queen, Prince James had melted into the sea of people. I didn't blame him. We were nobodies and rather boring ones at that. Surely, he'd had more than enough of our company.

Astrid smiled and playfully swatted my arm. "I cannot be-lieve we're here, Presti. This is the most amazing thing ever. And how nice is the prince? Not a hint of snobbery about him."

We stood before an enormous painting, by whom I did not

know, but it certainly wouldn't have been out of place in a gallery. "No. No snobbery at all."

"We mustn't latibulate, Presti. We should make an effort to meet people while we're here. People other than those at our table." Astrid ignored the painting, her attention fixed on the mass of attendees milling about the room.

Usually, hiding in a corner didn't bother me, but Astrid was right. This was a once-in-a-lifetime experience, so we had to make the most of it. We walked together, smiling and nodding hello to others, each searching for a friendly face we could claim and strike up a conversation with.

"Well, here we are, James. These guests were at your table, were they not?" A booming voice sounded from my left.

Turning to look—telling myself it was because the voice was so loud and definitely not because I'd heard the name James—I found myself face to face once more with Prince James. He stood amidst a small group who all stared at Astrid and me.

"That's right, George. This is Prestidigitation Jones and his good friend Astrid Rhys-Bomalier. Presti, Astrid. My brother, His Royal Highness Prince George."

Bowing to Prince George, the nerves that had assaulted me upon meeting James and, to a lesser extent, the queen, did not materialise with James's brother. "Good evening," I said smoothly.

"Ah, yes. Braxton told me all about this fellow. Kissed your hand, eh, James." Prince George and Braxton laughed riotously, quickly joined by his companion I'd yet to be introduced to and, after a moment's hesitation and some flustering, his brother James.

Heat burned my cheeks and spread to my ears until I

thought I might actually be aflame. What I had done might well be worthy of being laughed at, but the decent thing to do would be to do it behind my back. Astrid's hand slipped into mine, giving me a gentle squeeze. God, I loved her.

"Yes," Braxton said into the lessening laughter. "And during dinner he blurted something about glass buttocks."

Prince George laughed so hard I thought he was at risk of tears. James's gaze dashed to mine, wide and worried, then back to his brother. James gave a small chuckle, which I let myself believe seemed forced. It didn't matter though. Whether he meant the laughter or not, it appeared his manners had ended with our meal.

"Excuse us," I muttered, turned, and fled, practically dragging Astrid behind me.

"Well," said Astrid once we'd reached the other end of the music room, "what an utter dick."

"Mm," I grunted, not wanting to talk about it. The heat of shame hadn't cooled. Though I'd never see these people again and I didn't care what they thought of me, nobody likes to be laughed at to their face.

Chapter Four

I COULD HAVE decked George. Of course, I was angrier with myself than my knucklehead brother. Maybe Presti's social skills weren't as polished as some, but I'd found him quite delightful. I'd never met anyone like him before. From knowing some interesting facts and blurting out whatever thought seemed to be passing through his head at any given moment to his enthusiasm for the natural world and coexisting with it, I found him quite refreshing and downright beguiling.

Everything he felt, I could read in his incredible blue eyes. His embarrassment when he'd thanked me for coming and kissed my hand, his adoration for his mother and friends, his horror yet slight amusement when he'd blurted the tale of glass bottoms. All of it was written and so easily read on his handsome face. Unlike me, he was an open book.

While I could tell myself that only his personality drew me

to him, the simple fact was that Presti was stunning to look at. And I mean beautiful in a take-your-breath-away manner. Curly coal-black hair, bright-blue eyes, flawless skin aside from a birthmark shaped not unlike a turtle high on his left cheek, and the most kissable lips I'd ever seen. Despite the ill-fitting tux, it was plain to see his body beneath was fantastic — tall, trim, narrow waist, a swimmer's body. Add to that, great hands and a spectacular arse. Prestidigitation Jones was as close to perfect as anyone I'd ever met.

When I'd first locked eyes with his brilliant-blue ones, I felt a little as if the ground beneath me had dropped away. For the last few hours, I felt as if I were teetering on a shard of earth, waiting for an inevitable fall. I had no idea what any of that meant. But a strong pull of inevitability made me confident I could not escape whatever fate had in store. Not now that Presti had swept into my life.

And I'd just chased him away by laughing at him alongside my brother like we were a couple of frat boys bullying the school nerd. *Ugh.* All the kudos I gave myself for being better than George, and it turns out, I'm worse. At least George isn't afraid to be himself, even if he is a gigantic dick.

"Excuse me," I muttered, ambling away from George and his posse. I'd thought Hannah was to be George's date this evening, but she was nowhere in sight. It was a great shame, because she alone managed to curb George's boorish behaviour. She made him at least tolerable to be around.

George and Hannah had been dating for a little under twelve months. The press and the people adored her. If George somehow managed to marry her, she'd be twice as popular as the rest of us. I wish she'd been here tonight. George never would have openly mocked Presti, and I never would have been a giant prig and joined him.

As much as I detested my brother's behaviour, I saved my true ire for myself.

"All right, James?" Harlan asked when I practically ran him down in my attempt to escape my brother.

"Sorry, Harlan. Wasn't paying attention. Thinking about your sister, actually."

Harlan squinted, pushed his glasses up his nose and said, "Shame she couldn't make it tonight."

"I was just thinking the same. She's okay though?"

"Oh yes. Had a prior engagement." Harlan's gaze travelled the room, his feet shifting awkwardly. Unlike his sister, Hannah, Harlan had rather intense social anxiety. His presence here tonight without Hannah as his shield was something of a miracle.

"Are you okay, Harlan? I know events of this kind aren't your thing."

Harlan snorted. "Not at all. Must get used to them, I suppose. If George and Hannah… Well, you know." Harlan waved his hand about. I did know. Both families wanted them to marry. However, Harlan's family consisted only of grandparents and an uncle or two.

George desperately wanted Hannah to say yes, but I knew she had doubts. She feared becoming part of the royal family, but not for herself.

Hannah loved her brother, and she'd told me several times that she worried about him becoming a more public figure if she were to marry Prince George. Heir to the throne. This is yet another reason she'd be a perfect future queen. She did care for others.

"At least I knew everyone at my table," Harlan continued. "No mortifying first introductions. How was your table?"

Just then, Prestidigitation Jones walked across my line of sight. Astrid walked at his side, their arms linked, heads inclined toward each other as they chatted. The flush in his cheeks had faded, but as he lifted his head and caught my gaze, I noticed the sparkle in his eyes was gone too.

I'd contributed to that. No. I'd caused that.

And I couldn't stand that.

"Quite interesting, actually," I managed to reply. "I'd like you to meet some of them, Harlan. If you're up to it?"

"Ah, sure, I guess." Harlan glanced about nervously, but I was convinced he'd enjoy the company of Presti and Astrid. At least, that was the excuse I was giving myself for the chance to speak to Presti again. And apologise to him.

Presti watched us approach. His stunning eyes darted about, and I knew he was searching for an escape. How could I blame him after the way I behaved with George? While Presti looked ready to run, Astrid stood tall and proud, ready to bite my head off. I'd let her do it too. I deserved it.

"Presti, Astrid," I began as soon as we reached them. "I'd like to introduce you to Harlan Spence, the Earl of Fenwick."

"Hullo," Harlan said, offering his hand.

A ridiculous sensation shook my body as Presti reached to shake Harlan's hand. I wondered if he'd kiss Harlan's hand too. I was jealous. Ludicrously jealous that Presti might press his lips to another man's skin. What in the hell was wrong with me?

Presti merely shook Harlan's hand and offered a warm smile and a simple nice to meet you. Astrid did likewise. Then, she immediately began regaling Harlan with her feelings about his work with animal rights. Harlan was most famous for defending the rights of our animal friends. Well, at least that had been his claim to fame until Hannah and George began dating. And the longer they dated, the more serious their relationship became, and the more scrutiny Harlan and Hannah would face. Now, his life would become fodder for gossip; the more salacious, the better. Nobody seemed to care if it was true or not.

While Astrid swept Harlan up in talk about animals, I turned my attention to Prestidigitation Jones.

Perfect.

My plan was working perfectly. Plan? I only lacked the handlebar moustache to twirl with my fingers.

I turned to Presti, who stood stiffly, studiously avoiding my gaze. Yep. He was pissed or worse, hurt.

"Presti?"

He glanced my way before returning his gaze to Astrid and Harlan. "Mm?"

"Ah…I'd like to show you Gran's clock room. If you'd like, that is."

"Clock room?" he asked, interest spiked. The little curious twitch in his gaze was adorable.

"Yes. Gran has received many clocks as official gifts over the years. She keeps them all in the clock room. It's quite fascinating."

Presti turned and eyed me cautiously as if considering if he'd be safe with me. I hated that I'd planted that doubt in him. Despite his apparent hesitation in having anything more to do with me, I could read his expression well enough to know he desperately wanted to see this clock room.

"Clocks," Presti murmured. "A room full of clocks. How could I possibly say no to that." And then he smiled at me, warm and expansive, lighting him up like a bonfire. Brilliant.

"Very well, then. This way." I motioned toward the door leading to the south hallway. Presti led, and I fell into step behind him. My hand gently rested on the small of his back as I guided him out of the music room.

My life may not be my own, but I still found alone time — that time I often used to curl up with a good book. Sometimes, these books weren't so good but most had several things in common. A tingle or a spark when someone touched someone they were attracted to. I'd always considered it artistic fancy, but I'd have sworn on my life that my fingers tingled as they brushed Presti's body, even though he was most definitely fully clothed. And earlier, when my leg had fallen against his, it had been as if they'd been glued together. I'd been unable, or maybe unwilling, to separate from the feel of him.

"You know, a wonderful gentleman scientist once proposed a flower clock," Presti said as we exited the music room.

"A flower clock?"

"Mm, indeed. It would utilise the characteristic petal opening and closing times for various species of flowers. In effect, one could look out at one's garden and be able to tell the time based on which flowers were in bloom. Quite splendid, really."

"Quite. Gran does not have something quite so marvellous. She does have many unique timepieces though."

We walked the long corridor of the palace seemingly alone,

though I knew security agents wouldn't be too far behind us. Outside the door of my rooms, I was rarely truly alone. Always wondering who was watching or listening and what they'd do with whatever they saw or heard. I never truly relaxed. It was a hard way to live.

As I opened the door to the clock room, Presti's soft breath and earthy scent filled my senses. The soft ticking of the clocks couldn't compete with my thundering heartbeat. Though hundreds of clocks filled the room, Prestidigitation Jones overwhelmed me. He surrounded me until I felt filled with a gentle yearning.

"Wow!" Presti gasped, entering the room, his head shifting as he attempted to take in the view. "There must be a hundred clocks in here."

"Two hundred and forty-seven, actually."

"Does the queen have a thing for clocks — not like a kink, of course." Presti's face flamed that delicious red. "Not that the queen couldn't have a kink; I mean, you're here. Evidence that she isn't virginal." Presti's face scrunched in an adorable wince.

I couldn't drag my gaze from his beautiful face and pretty lips. I'd watched those lips all night twist around the words Presti spoke. I've never seen lips more obviously begging to be kissed. "Christ, but you are beautiful," I exclaimed.

Despite being in a room filled with clocks, time seemed to stop at my exclamation.

Presti's blue eyes watched me, squinting as though trying to puzzle me out. "Are you mocking me?" he asked.

"No. God, no. I'm so sorry about before, with George — I shouldn't have laughed. The fact is, Presti, that I like you. I quite like you very much." I meant the apology, but although liking Presti was the truth, I hadn't meant to tell him. Something about Presti somehow made keeping it to myself impossible.

Presti drew himself to his full height and said, "The apology would have sufficed. You don't need to embellish any fond feelings for me. I know I'm not… Well, people tend not to like me too much."

Taking a steadying breath, I stepped forward. His skin felt warm and soft where my hand cupped his cheek. I smiled when he tilted his head, leaning into my touch. "Then people are crazy, because you are adorable, Prestidigitation Jones. You are unlike anyone I've ever met, and I've met many people."

"I do t-tend to get called odd a fair bit," Presti stammered. Though I could feel him trembling, his gaze never left mine.

"I should very much like to kiss you," I whispered. Another confession I'd thought to keep to myself. Yet, for some reason, I couldn't help but blurt out these little titbits of feelings.

Presti answered with a slight nod of his head. I leaned in a fraction closer, our bodies so close I felt the warmth of his, yet he didn't reach for me. "You can say no, Presti. I shan't send you to the Tower for it."

His blue eyes softened, those gorgeous lips twisting into a small smile. "You've quite bewitched me, Prince James. I can't think of a single thing I want more in this moment than a kiss…from you."

Those words, that permission, were all I needed. I pressed my lips to his softly, tenderly. I pulled away and sighed at the tingle cascading along my spine from that simple kiss. Then Presti's hand gripped my waist, tentative at first, and then more firmly.

I kissed him again, deeper, more urgent. My mouth moved with his as I tasted him, revelled in the feel of his body pressing against mine. The want grew between us, teetering on the edge of need.

How could I need someone I'd only just met?

As his tongue met mine in a shy dance, the feeling of nothing ever being the same again grew and twisted inside me. I'd stumbled upon a vine of hope that maybe I could find someone to share my life with, and it was wrapping me up inside. Reality would soon enough shatter all my Prestidigitation fantasies. Just for now, I'd let myself have them, have him.

"Wow," Presti murmured as I dragged my lips from his to press soft, open-mouthed kisses along the column of his neck.

"Wow, indeed." I wanted to taste every inch of him. I wanted to spend hours with him, trying to drag out more of those soft moans I doubted he even realised he let escape. "I think it is you who has bewitched me."

"Must have been all that talk about your grandmother's kinks," Presti said. He stiffened in my arms. "Oh, sorry. That was awfully unflirtatious. Let me try again."

Try as I might, I couldn't contain a chuckle. "How do you do it?" I asked, pulling him closer, refusing to yield him from my hold even a little.

"Do what?" he squeaked as I nibbled on his ear lobe.

"Just be yourself," I mumbled.

"I don't know how to be anything else."

My lips found his again, his taste exploding on my tongue. Lust and longing boiled in my veins, but there was no way I would go any further with Presti in my gran's clock room, much as I wanted to.

"Ahem," a booming voice ripped me from the best kiss I'd ever shared. It was a voice I knew well. And the very last one I wanted to hear when I was in the arms of a man.

"Father," I muttered. Presti and I stood together, shoulders brushing as we faced the next King of England, my father.

"So, it's true then," my father replied, glaring at me as he studiously avoided shifting his gaze to Presti.

My father wasn't homophobic; in fact, he did a great deal in support of the LGBT community. It was just there'd never been a queer senior royal before. It was one of the many reasons I'd never come out or had a boyfriend. I barely had a sex life. Who could I trust to keep my great secret? How could I be sure they wouldn't go running to the tabloids to tell — sell — my story?

Fear had kept me from forming any meaningful relationship with anybody. However, that wasn't entirely true. The truth was I'd never met anybody I'd been willing to risk exposure for — until now.

"Father — "

"Good evening, Your Highness," Presti cut in. "Please forgive me for kissing your son. Entirely my fault. A great misunderstanding, I think. Quite accidental."

"Accidental?" My father smirked. "One of those 'I tripped and fell onto his lips 'type of situations, then?"

"Quite. You see, James, ah rather, His Royal Highness, was showing me his grandmother's clocks — actually, you may be fascinated to know that the world's oldest working clock is right here in England. Salisbury Cathedral, to be exact." Presti stilled and tilted his head a little as he looked at my father. "Though I expect you likely know that being the future king and all. Probably not much you don't know about your realm. Anyhoo, I should best be re-joining my friend, Astrid. She's positively wonderful, but she does tend to talk a person's ear off once she gets riled up about a topic. I'd hate to think she was assaulting a royal ear right now. So, bye-bye now. So delightful to meet you both. Bye-bye."

And with that, Presti dashed out of the room.

My father watched him flee before turning back to me with a grin. "Well, he was…certainly interesting."

"Father, I—"

"James." My father held his hand up to silence me. "We'll discuss this tomorrow. Make a plan. For now, we both need to return to the party."

I silently followed my father back down the hall, glaring at my security man, though I was not sure what I expected him to do. Stop my father from barging in and ruining the best kiss of my life? How could he even have known there was a chance I'd be kissing a man behind that door? Nobody knew.

But they did now. My father knew my big secret. And apparently, we were going to make a plan on how to handle it. Great. I couldn't wait.

Chapter Five

PRESTI, COME ON," Astrid whined.

From the moment I'd rushed back to her side, colliding impressively with Harlan, Earl of Somewhere or Other, Astrid had begged me to divulge what had happened. She wanted to know what had sent me fleeing, red-faced and horribly mortified, from the presence of Prince James.

How could I tell her? What could I tell her? James's sexuality wasn't my secret to share. But I'd never kept anything from Astrid before. Even my only sexual encounter, which had ended in the unfortunate destruction of one-third of a two-hundred-year-old, historically listed home I had shared with Astrid. Every painfully humiliating minute, including my rescue — sans clothes — by a local fireman who also moonlighted as a weekend supervisor at the paper towel factory where I worked. I'd told her all.

Astrid knew everything about me. But I'd clammed up

when she'd asked a second, third, and now fourth time what had happened with Prince James. My lips were sewn shut, so to speak.

Now, here we were, the morning after the night before and still she asked. And still, I remained resolute. I didn't want to tell her that the most amazing experience I'd ever shared with a man was over. Happened and ended so quickly. Nor did I wish to admit I considered it a very good chance the best moment I'd ever have had come and gone. Over. Leaving me with nothing but a life of mediocrity to face. What or who could ever compare to the kiss I'd shared with James? There was a slim chance I was prone to dramatise things, but that kiss was amazing.

And Prince James… Well, I just couldn't, with his wonderfully ginger-caramel hair, slightly scruffy beard, and those teal-green eyes that reminded me so much of a mix between forests and oceans. Dreamy.

"Was there some kind of curfuggle you became embroiled in? Right there in Her Majesty's Wunderkammer. Tell me you didn't break one of her clocks," Astrid pressed. She leaned across the small balcony table we sat at, the London vista spread out before us bathed in the pinks and oranges of early morning light. Her cool fingers brushed my cheek. "Won't you tell me, Presti?"

I wanted to share this burden with her, but how could I betray James? "There was something of a mess," I stammered. "A small misunderstanding with Prince Arthur."

"James's father?"

"Mm. That's the one."

"He seems something of a curmudgeon. He didn't shout at you for being in a part of the palace not meant for plebeian eyes, did he?"

I loved how Astrid sounded so ready to march back to the palace to defend me against the future king if he had yelled at me. "Oh, you wonderful creature. No, he didn't yell at me. I simply felt awkward caught alone with James is all."

Astrid raised a quizzical brow, dissatisfied with my answer, so I continued, "I went on a bit of a verbal rant. Just the usual."

My dearest friend continued eyeing me rather disbelievingly, but she said, "Very well. I shall leave it at that for now, but when you're ready to talk about it, I'm here." Astrid stood and turned to go back through the balcony doors into our room.

She stopped with one foot already through the threshold. "I don't know if this will help or not," Astrid began, "but after you returned from the clock room, Prince James could not take his eyes off you."

And then she left me, my mouth agape, strawberry jam-topped muffin in hand. But how could I eat after that unlikely proclamation? She had to have imagined the entire thing.

Several hours later, I found myself dragging my feet in utter exhaustion as Mum, Howard, Astrid, and I attempted to see all the sights of London that we could squeeze into a twenty-four-hour period. Technically, we had three more days here, but there was just so much to see.

"Those guards do look rather resplendent, do they not?" Astrid asked as we stood at the gates of the palace. It was hard to believe that less than twenty-four hours ago, we'd been behind these gates, inside the walls of Buckingham Palace, hobnobbing with no less than queens, future kings and noble folk of all kinds.

"They're bearskin, dear," my mother answered.

"Beg pardon?"

"Their hats. Black bearskins."

Astrid stared at Mum and glared back at the guards, and I braced myself for what was to come. "Slaughterers," she cried. "Have you no souls? These gentle creatures are our brothers and sisters, and you would wear their skins as a hat?" Astrid clutched the fence bars surrounding the palace, rattling them as she snarled at the guards.

"Astrid, dear," my mother soothed. "I'm so sorry I've upset you."

"You were merely the bearer of this grotesque news, Mrs Jones. One cannot go through life ignorant of such abominable circumstances."

While I'm not sure I would have agreed with Astrid's description of bears as gentle creatures, I concurred with her assessment of the situation. Humanity was a bottomless pit of cruelty towards the innocent creatures of our planet, to say nothing of what we did to each other.

Before I could utter a word, Astrid leapt on the bars of the palace fence, still rattling them—at least trying to—while hurling expletives toward the hapless, bearskin-festooned guards the whole time.

A crowd soon gathered, some quickly joining Astrid once they understood her protest. Mum and Howard stood nearby, smiling fondly at Astrid.

Just as I made to join my friend upon the battlefield, my phone rang. Without even looking at the screen, I answered, "Hello?"

"Presti?"

"Speaking. Who's this?"

"James."

"James?" I could hardly hear my caller with the spontaneous protesters shouting and ranting around me. Had they said James? Was it *that* James?

"James, Prince James."

"Oh, *that* James," I replied rather awkwardly. "For some reason, I didn't expect royalty to make their own phone calls. Perhaps you had a personal... Well, I don't know what that person would be called. Royal phone caller?" I mused.

"Um, no. I make my own calls, actually," James replied.

"So it would seem."

"May I ask where you are, Presti? Sounds awfully noisy there."

I shifted awkwardly. Did I want to admit to James that I was outside his home, engaged in a rapidly expanding protest against his family's guards? "Ah, about that—"

"Could you hold on a sec? There's a bit of noise where I am too. Let me close my window."

A few seconds later, James came back on the line. "Seems there's a protest going on here at the palace. No doubt whoever they are will be hauled away shortly."

"I see." I gulped, took a deep breath, and continued, "Funny thing. I'm in the middle of something of a protest myself."

"Really?" James asked.

"Mm. Astrid has started something, I'm afraid. She is rather good at riling people up for a good cause. Something of a talent."

"What on earth is she protesting?"

"Bearskins."

"Ah." A stunned silence fell over us before James continued,

"Um, Presti? You wouldn't happen to be outside Buckingham Palace right now, would you?"

"Actually, yes," I admitted. "Unfortunately, Mum chose a rather inopportune time to point out that the guards 'hats are bearskin. I'm afraid that doesn't sit well with Astrid at all. Nor me for that matter," I added, wanting to defend my friend and the bears simultaneously.

Soft chuckling tickled my ear as James said, "How wonderful you both are. I have been protesting that with Gran's advisors and general hangers-on for years."

"Really?"

"Nobody is remotely concerned with what upsets me, though." James's voice softened as he continued, "I'm thought of as something of an outcast. The press and my father have often said I'm trying to ruin the tradition of royalty."

My insides pinched as I listened to this misunderstood prince. "I don't believe that. I mean the part about you trying to ruin tradition. I think you're just like the rest of us."

Again, James's quiet laughter bubbled over the phone. "Just like the rest of you, huh?"

"Well, of course. We all want the same thing. Acceptance. To live our lives as we choose, peacefully and happily." Prince James may have money, travel the world, and live in palaces, but I didn't envy him for his life.

"How did you get so wise at such a young age, Presti?"

"Well, I—put her down! Just what in the Sam Hill do you think you're doing? Astrid! Astrid, for the love of everything, do not bite that man," I screeched. Astrid's protest had, unsurprisingly, devolved into chaos.

In the short time I'd spoken to James, the police had arrived and were trying to extricate Astrid from her firm grip on the palace fence bars. She, naturally, was snapping her teeth at them.

"Ah, Presti?" James's tinny phone voice shouted at me. I raised my mobile back to my ear.

"James. I must away, as it were."

"Tell me Astrid isn't biting the palace guards." Despite the topic, the prince's voice quivered with amusement.

"Oh, no. Not at all," I replied. "She's trying to bite the police. Bobbies, I believe is the term. I must look up where that came from. Bobbies." This would not be the first time Astrid and I became involved in an altercation with police during one of our protests. But we weren't at home this time. Home was thousands of kilometres away, and I had no idea how British police handled protesters, especially ones protesting outside the home of their beloved queen.

"Well, that's…better, I guess," James stammered. "Ah, I know you have to go and all, but I did call for a reason."

"Oh?" I asked, my curiosity piqued.

"Yes. I wondered, that is, I hoped you might join me for dinner this evening."

"Dinner?"

"Dinner. Here at the palace. You and me. Alone."

There was nothing for it. I was losing my mind. People like me did not get asked to dinner by princes. "Dinner," I stammered stupidly. "And we'll eat? Together."

"That is usually how dinner works." James laughed.

"But… but…" But what? I liked Prince James, and, goodness knows, he was possibly the most beautiful man I'd ever seen, but he was also a prince. Royalty. Men like me didn't—

"Presti! What the devil are you doing? We have a protest to conduct, and you're standing there lollygagging—wait, who are you talking to?"

"Miss, you need to come with us."

"I will not. Presti! Get off that phone." The rest of Astrid's plea for my help came out muffled as a policewoman tackled her to the ground.

"Ah, James, I really must go, but I would, well, I would simply lovetohavedinnerwith you," I blurted, running my words together before James could change his mind. "Get off her. This instant!"

I dove for my friend, unsure of my plan but knowing I could not allow this bobby to manhandle her—were female officers bobbies also? Like that mattered right now. My phone flew from my hand, landing…somewhere. I didn't have time to worry that Prince James remained on the line. Would he listen to the cacophony as more police arrived, pulling at me as I wrestled one of their own off Astrid?

Astrid continued shouting, "Save the bears." A chorus of voices joining her from the crowd amassed around us. From my position, flat on my back, one bobby on my legs while another all but sat on my chest, I saw my mother swat at more officers with her handbag.

It seemed we'd started something of an all-in brawl. The hiss and whirr of camera shutters warned me we would likely end up on YouTube. Maybe even the news. Prince James, I was confident, would not appreciate that at all.

There went my dinner date, I lamented while trying to dislodge the bulk of an officer from my chest. As much as I liked James, I was pretty sure the poor bears were more important—I didn't think he was in immediate danger of being made into a hat. How much could I possibly mean to James anyway? We'd spent a few hours together. Chances were phenomenally high that he would forget he'd ever met Prestidigitation Jones in a matter of days.

And why did that thought provoke a slight ache in my chest?

"Presti," my mother called. "Oh, do get off him. Presti? Are you all right? I said get off him. He's only a wee little lad." She glared at the bobby sitting astride me.

Cringing at my mother's unfortunate turn of phrase in describing me, I continued my struggle. Astrid roared at my side, bellowing her chant but mixing in a few expletives directed toward law enforcement.

As the chaos rattled toward its inevitable peak, all about me suddenly fell quiet, a hush settling amongst what had seconds ago been a fiery protest. For a moment, I pondered whether one of the police officers had drawn a weapon. But the atmosphere felt unthreatening. More awed than hostile.

Low murmurs drifted on the cool, crisp air. I'd been warned London would be freezing this time of year, but an unseasonal warmth kept temperatures in the mid-teens. Cold, but hardly freezing.

Try as I might, I couldn't quite make out the words people whispered around me.

Suddenly, the weight pressing on my chest eased as the bobby struggled to his feet. I watched as his skin paled and his eyes boggled. Then he bowed low. "Your Royal Highness," he mumbled.

Royal Highness? Surely not.

"May I ask what is going on here?" James's voice, low and threatening, sent a spike of yearning straight up my spine. What the devil was he doing here?

"Arresting some protesters, Your Highness."

James glanced down at me. And winked. It was entirely un- fair that he appeared so devastatingly handsome and put-to- gether while I lay flat on my back, sprawled like a sack of pota- toes. And then he had the audacity to wink at me so relaxed and calmly while I sweated bullets of nerves.

"They're protesting... Well, about bears, I think." The poor bobby looked thoroughly flummoxed. I guess when the poor fel- low awoke this morning, he hadn't expected his day to go quite along these lines.

"Bears? Hmm." James favoured me with a second wink and then reached a hand down to me.

Without a thought, I took it and allowed the prince of Eng- land to haul me to my feet. As I glanced around, my cheeks pinkening as all eyes settled on me, I noticed Astrid smiling rather proudly at me. My mother and Howard stood at her side, the three watching me with smugness and surprise.

"You know," James said, his gaze fixed on me but clearly addressing the crowd, my hand still wrapped firmly in his. "It is quite a barbaric practice, this making our guards 'hats out of bear- skin. The queen and I have spoken about this several times and intend to take action."

A loud cheer rose from the crowd. I had no idea if it was true, but the crowd loved James for it. And I knew it was what he wanted. Putting aside his moral fortitude in standing up for what was right, he looked positively dashing doing it. Of course, my mature side was far more impressed with his actions. But, oh hell, I could not deny how gorgeous he looked with the midday sun highlighting the copper flecks in his hair, the light illuminating his teal irises, so they looked something like the calm waters of the Aegean—at least pictures I'd seen of it. I found Prince James irresistibly enchanting.

"What are you doing, James?" I whispered, finally wriggling my fingers free from his.

"I believe," he began, his lovely mouth upturned in a mischievous grin," I am being chivalrous. Coming to the rescue and all that."

Heat burned beneath my skin, flushing my face all shades of red. This man may well be the death of me.

Before I could wrestle a reply from my mouth, Astrid threw herself at the prince, squeezing her arms so tightly about him that I feared he could scarcely breathe. "You wonderful man. If only all royalty were as noble." Astrid beamed.

"Astrid, dear," my mother cut in, "I think you're making Prince James's poor bodyguards very nervous."

Only then did I notice the two large men fidgeting tensely, hands twitching around the area where I suspected they had their weapons secreted. How close were we to a regrettable incident? The taller of the two men seemed only seconds from drawing a gun and shooting my friend.

"I think Mother might be on to something, Astrid. Might I suggest backing slowly away from the royal personage," I murmured, afraid any loud noise might ignite the spark.

Prince James laughed. Easy enough for him, I suppose; it wasn't his head in the firing line. "It's quite all right. Billy and Gordon are under strict orders not to pull their weapons today."

"Good to know," Howard replied as he handed me my phone.

"Presti?" James asked when Astrid finally released her grip upon him. "Are you okay?"

"Well, it's a lot…all this, I mean," I exclaimed, waving my arms about quite maniacally. "One doesn't encounter situations like this in Kincumber."

"Wonderfully odd name that, Kincumber," James replied.

"Huh," I huffed. "I hardly think you can comment on our place names when you have a village here in England called Blubberhouses."

James stared a moment before bursting into laughter. "We do? I had no idea. Blubberhouses," he snorted. "You are extraordinary, Presti."

Over the years, I'd learned when I was being laughed at. This was not one of those times. Prince James of England found me extraordinary. I didn't know what to do with that.

Chapter Six

MY GOD, I found Prestidigitation Jones completely mesmerising. I'd been attracted to men before, naturally. Admired their hard planes and sculptured physiques. I'd felt the sharp spike of desire looking at a chiselled jaw or a neatly kept beard. I'd never experienced this warm, fluttery feeling before. The last twenty-four hours had been… Actually, I didn't know quite how to describe my life since Presti had delightfully barged into it.

Since my birth, palace courtiers, hangers-on, and yes-men have surrounded me. Presti couldn't have been more unlike them with his genuine warmth, his sincere interest in the world around him. Entirely unafraid to be himself, he was completely unlike me.

His gorgeous blue eyes sparkled in the sunlight, crinkling as he laughed with me. He was so enchanting when he chuckled that I forgot what we were laughing at. Not that it mattered. I was content to watch Presti.

I could have watched him all day. However, Billy would hustle me back inside the palace walls any minute. Or worse, somebody would inform my father, and he would not be pleased. Father and I had briefly chatted this morning before he'd been called away with some future monarch emergency. We hadn't even come close to planning for my coming out or whatever we were going to do now that he knew I was gay.

Ugh, just thinking about coming out had bile rising in my gut. The world was progressing in its acceptance of queer folk, but let's be honest, the road was still rocky. And first to be out as a gay senior royal would be a pressure I wasn't sure I could or wanted to handle.

Yet here I stood, in full view of the public, defending and making googly eyes at the first man who'd piqued my interest in years. Maybe even ever. And there he stood, staring back at me with an expression I couldn't quite decipher, yet I knew I wanted to watch it on his extraordinary face for a long, long time. Was it wonder? Interest?

My skin heated, sweat beading on my forehead. My entire body felt as if I were suddenly made of jelly. My stomach lurched as reality gut punched me. What the hell was I doing? Any second now, people would see through the inch-thick steel walls I'd built around myself. They'd notice the way Presti and I were…ogling each other. My god, I'd practically been holding hands with him.

I felt sick and shaky as if the ground were rising to greet me. I couldn't faint. I just couldn't. All the Presti-induced bravado that had dragged my sorry arse out from behind palace walls evaporated in an instant. Leaving me with nothing but cold, stark terror.

"No charges, please," I addressed the police, ignoring

completely the wonderful man who, only seconds ago, I thought I'd never be able to turn away from. "Good day to you all."

And then I was gone, running for the safety of the palace. Behind me, I heard the crowd's murmurs mixed with Billy and Gordon's heavy breaths as they dashed to keep up with me. I knew running only added to the spectacle I had already made of myself, but I needed to get far from Presti. Quickly. As far as I could before I screwed everything up and kissed him smack on the lips like I wanted.

Jesus. I couldn't breathe, and it had nothing to do with the fast pace I'd set to get me back to the palace. London had put on a bright blue sky, the air crisp and fresh, but I felt trapped as if in a small, dark box. Not enough air reached my lungs. I tried sucking in huge gulps, but it didn't feel enough.

Completely lost to my panic, it hardly registered when Billy or Gordon grabbed my arm and dragged me the remaining few metres into the palace. My knees hit the carpeted floor as I struggled to draw breath.

"Your Highness?" one of my protection officers asked. I couldn't tell who, but I could hear the other one talking rapidly, his words nothing but fuzzy white noise.

"I'm…" I stammered. "I'm all right."

Billy knelt at my side, his worried gaze checking me over. "We've got the palace nurse coming, Your Highness. Sit tight."

I shook my head. "Not necessary."

"With all due respect, Your Highness, I disagree. Please. Let the nurse check you over." Billy and Gordon had been my protection officers since I was a small boy. I trusted them. I liked them. But I knew they had to report this afternoon's events, and I knew they'd have their arses kicked if I didn't see the nurse. There'd be enough trouble for letting me outside the grounds unannounced. I couldn't let them get in any more trouble because of my actions.

"All right. But let me get to my rooms," I bargained.

Twenty minutes later, I lay in the sanctuary of my private suite. The nurse had left only five minutes ago, satisfied I'd only suffered a panic attack and was otherwise quite well. All that remained was the expected visit from my father. And for me to figure out what I would do about Presti.

After an hour, I began to think my father wasn't coming. The television in my room offered the only light as the night sky set in. I'd turned the volume low, but my eyes scanned the screen as I flicked through the news stations. I'd been sure I'd see a newsflash spilling my great secret to the world, so sure I'd see footage of Presti and me holding hands, staring into each other's eyes.

Gordon had brought me a cup of tea a while ago, but it remained untouched and cooling on my side table. The thought of food curdled my stomach. I was a mess.

"James?" My father edged hesitantly toward me. I hadn't even heard him knock on my door. "James. What happened?"

With that simple question, the dam inside me burst, and the cork that had kept me silent since my return to the palace popped. "What happened? Father, I went out…out of the palace where they were protesting. The bearskins, the hats. You know, I've often spoken of them. I went out there because of Presti. He was there, and I… He was so close, and I wanted to see him. I also didn't want him hauled off to jail. But we held hands, sort of and—"

I shook my head and fought for the right words, but before

I could continue, my father said, "Breathe, James. Take a deep breath. You're okay now."

Years had passed since I'd last hugged my father or been hugged by him. But I flew into his arms, calmed by his strength, his warmth. Tears pricked my eyes, but I held them back, wouldn't let them fall. Not because I believed men shouldn't cry but because I was deathly afraid if I cried, I'd never stop.

My father held me until I felt as if I could finally breathe normally again. He led me to a sofa and eased me down. "I've seen the footage," he murmured as he sat opposite me. "I don't think it's going to be as big a problem as you think."

"Really?" Could I have blown the whole incident out of proportion? Had I built a mountain out of nothing but a molehill?

Father's gaze flittered about the room, refusing to land on mine. "Father, please. Don't lie to me," I begged. Prince Arthur, the future king of England, my father, was many things. A good liar wasn't one of them.

Sighing heavily, my father said, "All right. To be honest, I don't think it's so bad, but Simon is in a bit of a flap about it. He's got your gran worked up, and she's talking to George about…"

"About what?"

"About proposing to Hannah. Well, I guess he's already done that. It's more pressing for her to answer. She loves your brother, but she's worried about her own."

"I know that, Father. She shouldn't have to rush into a decision just because…" Because I'd forgotten myself in public, and now, we were searching for some big news to attract attention away from me, from what I'd done. What was bigger and better than a royal engagement?

"No. She shouldn't be rushed. But your brother deserves an answer too. If it's a no, then he needs to move on. Find himself someone else." My parents had a happy marriage; at least, it appeared to be. In fairness, I rarely saw them together these days. Perhaps distance was the secret to their happiness.

Mother did enough charity work for seven princesses. She was somewhere in Africa right now. The push to marry off George mainly was to ensure the royal line continued, but I knew our parents also wanted George and me to be happy in our marriages.

"So, Simon's hoping George's big announcement will sideline my bungle," I sighed.

"Forget all that for a second, James. Tell me what you want."

Slowly, I raised my eyes to my father. "I asked Presti to have dinner with me tonight. Before…before that disaster out there."

"So, you want Presti?" my father asked as though it were the simplest thing in the world.

"I've never known anyone like him. And he makes me feel… I'm all fluttery and warm when I'm near him." I held my father's stare, waiting for judgement, maybe some mocking.

"Then you should have dinner with him."

"I… I made such a fool of myself running away from him. I don't know if I can do this." The weight of my admission sat heavily on my shoulders. Was I a coward for being afraid to let go of my big secret?

The truth struck me like a thunderbolt. As much as I liked Presti, I didn't know him well enough to decide if he was worth outing myself for. Did that make me an awful person? I just didn't know.

"James," my father murmured, "I haven't always been the best father; I know that. I was brought up on duty, a life of service. But I hope you know I will always be on your side." He kissed the top of my head, something he hadn't done in years.

Those damn tears pricked at my eyes again. "What about Gran?" I asked, knowing her approval or disapproval could make all the difference.

"Your gran is—" My father sighed heavily. "—from a different era. This won't be so easy for her to accept, but she loves you, James. She'll come around in the end."

"Okay." I nodded.

"Think it through. It can be done without drawing attention if you want to see your young man tonight. All right?"

"All right. Thank you, Father."

"Good. Good." My father stood and drew in a deep breath. "Well, I think that's quite enough parenting for me for one day. We'll talk later. Yes?"

"Yes."

And then he left. Went back to the world of being the future king, no doubt, and leaving me alone with the turmoil of my raging thoughts and indecisive mind. Though I couldn't deny it surprised me, it helped to know my father was on my side, but I still didn't know what I wanted to do.

From my window, I couldn't see the crowd of protesters. I hoped the police had listened to me and not charged any of them. The idea that Presti might, this second, be being arrested and hauled away by police made me ill. I told myself I'd feel that way about anybody, but who was I kidding? I liked Presti more than I should.

I stood in uncharted territory. I'd never been interested in getting to know somebody before. Dating had never held much appeal for me. Prestidigitation Jones had, in less than twenty-four hours, tipped my world on its axis.

There was nothing to be done but call him. Again.

Presti didn't answer. Not the first time I called him, nor the second. Did it make me desperate and pathetic if I called him a third time? Or did it just show that I was concerned about a friend? Were Presti and I friends? I'd shared one meal and about four hours in total with him.

Ugh, my head was so mixed up.

So lost was I in the field of chaos in my mind that it didn't immediately register with me when my phone rang. When it did, the ringing shocked me out of my stupor enough that I almost dropped the phone. Instead, I slammed it against my ear to answer it so hard that I was certain to bruise.

"Hello," I barked.

"James?"

Presti. He was calling me. Well, he was returning my calls, actually, but I wasn't about to argue over the finer points. Presti called me.

"James? Are you there? I don't think he's there, Astrid. I told you they were likely butt dials." Presti's voice wobbled, a nervous tremor streaking through it. "I'm quite sure the palace does not have a doorbell, Mother. Even if it did, I'd be stopped by those palace guards before I got anywhere near the front door. Wha —no, Astrid, I will not wrestle one of the offending hats off the guard's head to make a spectacle of it all."

Laughter erupted out of me like a jolly Vesuvius. Presti had an uncanny ability to make me smile, laugh, and feel free in a way I never did. "Presti, I'm here."

"Oh, you are there. I suspected I was speaking to your butt. Well, not your… You know what I mean."

"I do."

"I missed your call. Both of your calls, that is."

"Um, yeah," I stammered. The courage I'd felt moments ago after my father's apparent support of my interest in Presti fled. Dried up. Vanished. What would my life look like if I pursued Presti? What would it feel like if I didn't? "I wanted to apologise. For earlier. Disappearing on you like I did. I do hope none of you were arrested."

People should give me a white feather for my cowardice and be done with it. I was blathering like a fool instead of asking this man if he was still interested in having dinner with me. I knew in my guts I had no intention of repeating the invitation, and I hated myself for it.

"No. No, the bobbies left shortly after you did. Everything calmed down."

"Good. That's good." *Hello most awkward conversation ever.* "Well, I hope you enjoy the rest of your stay in England." I'm not sure I'd ever rolled my eyes at myself before, but I think they were close to rolling right out of my head.

For long seconds, Presti said nothing, which was awful. But then he said, "Thank you, Prince James. It was a very great pleasure to make your acquaintance." Which was so much worse.

Presti spoke politely, graciously, coldly. And I hated it. But I didn't know how to fix this. *Liar.*

"Well, I expect I'll see you in another twenty years for your grandmother's… Oh, what would that be? Eighty years on the throne? Oh, I see. Thank you, Astrid. Oak jubilee, Astrid tells me. I expect Her Majesty might receive some furniture as gifts or perhaps an oak forest. A lovely oak clock for her collection. She's very spritely for her age, so I don't expect she'll have any trouble…living that long," Presti rambled. The reminder of Gran's clock collection room and the kiss Presti and I shared in there wedged a sharp ache in my chest. Would it hurt forever? If so, I deserved the pain.

Though I'd known him a handful of hours, I realized rambling seemed to be Presti's default setting when upset or nervous. The kindest thing I could do was to end this conversation here and now. Let us both walk away with some dignity before any real damage. I was a prince of England, third in line to the throne, dammit. I had a position to live up to.

"Goodbye, Presti."

"Yes, of course. Goodbye, farewell and adieu. I—" And then Prestidigitation Jones was gone. He'd hung up before completing whatever he'd been about to utter.

In the split second when it registered that I may never see or speak to him again, I hated everything. Myself most of all.

Chapter Seven

THE PHONE IN my hand felt like a lead weight. I did not have a clue what had gone so wrong. Prince James had asked me to dinner mere hours—minutes—ago, and now he'd given me the brush-off. *It was nice to meet you. Now, return to the penal colony where we sent your kind only a hundred or so years ago.* I racked my brain, searching for how I had messed things up so quickly.

"Presti?" My mother's soft, I'm-worried-about-you voice broke through my ruminations.

Prince James had been in my life for a matter of hours. I shouldn't feel the sad aching in my breastbone because I knew I'd never see him again. My hands shouldn't be shaking at the loss of something…valuable.

Ridiculous.

Utterly ridiculous.

"Presti?" my mother murmured a second time.

"It was only Prince James, making certain we hadn't been arrested by the constabulary and…saying goodbye," I mumbled, entirely shaken by recent events. I had no business being so affected by a man I hardly knew.

"A very nice young man," Mother replied. "Seems quite untouched by his regal…ness?"

My mother was quite right if she meant James was no snob who looked down on his subjects. But I'd seen other ways that being royal had touched James, even in the short time I'd spent with him. I wondered if he'd ever spent a day in his life just simply being James rather than His Royal Highness.

A shudder ripped up my spine. James lived a life I could scarcely imagine and had no desire to. I should be relieved at the termination of our…whatever we'd had. Yet, all I felt was a powerful sense of loss.

"And that was all he wanted?" Astrid asked, her small hand gently squeezing my bicep.

"Yes. That was all he wanted," I murmured.

Though I hadn't shared anything about the kiss between James and me, and with the protest, I hadn't had a chance to mention the dinner invitation, Astrid knew me too well. I had no doubt she could feel my disappointment now James had rescinded the invite.

"Oh, Presti, this is not quite the fairy tale I envisaged for you." Astrid's kind eyes softened.

"I hardly knew him, As."

"That may be, but I… Well, I'm always hopeful for you, Presti."

Smiling, though I hardly felt happy, I replied, "One day, my prince shall come along, Astrid. It just so happens my prince is not *this* prince."

"Well, I must say I'm glad of it." Astrid smirked and winked. "Imagine if you'd married him—I simply refuse to curtsey to you, Prestidigitation Jones. Not when I've seen you in those garish fluorescent boxer shorts you so love to wear."

And just like that, Astrid pulled me from my funk.

"What is your problem with them? Ever since you spied them on the line and then on my person, you've had some inexplicable hatred toward them." As I spoke, I turned my back and began walking away from the palace, knowing my family would follow. They'd follow me through the fiery pits of Hades if I needed them to.

"They're just so bright," Astrid continued, falling into step at my side. "I suspect they could be spotted from the space station."

"Well, it does pay to advertise," Howard added. I didn't know whether to laugh or burn with shame.

So, I laughed. These people loved me no matter what. I didn't need to land a prince as my paramour to consider myself the luckiest person alive.

*

A DAY LATER, I once again sat on a great behemoth as QANTAS flight 2 flew us home. We'd seen as much of London as we could squeeze into our short time there. On day three of our travels, Howard had declared that if he was forced into one more church, he was bound to burst into flames.

I'd heard nothing more from Prince James. End of that

particular story, then.

Though there was still so much of the great city we hadn't seen, I was glad to head home. I'd travel again one day if I could, but Kincumber would always be home.

Despite her protests to the contrary, Astrid had indeed become one half of those grotesquely annoying couples who pined pathetically for each other if they endured a parting longer than a day. In Astrid's case, the pining for Larry did not take effect until the early morning of day four. Credit where it's due, I guess; she'd lasted longer than the last time they'd been separated.

As we soared high over the subcontinent in the endless blue sky, jealousy pierced my soul. I'd never been anything but happy for my mother and Astrid. They deserved the joy they both found due to their romantic partnerships. But for the first time, I had the oddest feeling. I wanted to experience that bliss.

"What are you excogitating over, Presti? You look quite perplexed."

"Hmm? Oh, I'm mostly thinking about you and Larry. Mother and Howard."

Astrid tilted her head as she often did when trying to figure me out. "Are you so very lonely, Presti?"

"Not lonely as such. I just… Maybe I'm ready to…not be so alone."

"I think that's marvellous. It'll be magnificent to double date with you and whatever lucky fellow snags your heart."

"What if…" I faltered, unsure how to express my worry, my fear. "What if there is no one out there for me?"

"Ridiculous," Astrid snorted. "Who could fail to love you, Presti? You are perfect."

A smile ticked my lips. I may be many things, but I knew perfect was not one of them. Besides, I didn't want to be perfect; I'd settle for being lovable. "I thought maybe… Well, Prince James seemed to like me. But, of course, I must have been quite mistaken."

"Prince James is a gigantic ignoramus, a total dorbellist. He may be devastatingly handsome, pleasant to confabulate with, and wealthy, but he suffers from a complete absence of sense."

A soft chuckle escaped me at my friend's defence of my honour. "It's a good thing we've left British airspace. I'm fairly certain you could be arrested for insulting a royal family member like that."

Astrid smiled and nuzzled into my arms. "I love you, Presti. The right man is out there for you. We must simply find him."

"Love you, too."

"Do you think some big fuss will be made on our return?" Astrid asked, steering me from further rumination on my lack of a love life.

I smiled, unable to help myself when I thought of the welcome home we'd receive from Larry, Astrid's father, and various friends of Mother's and Howard's. "Quite certain. Though I suspect Larry might spirit you away before too long."

Astrid sighed, that dreamy, faraway look drifting over her features. She looked radiant, as she did any time Larry starred in her thoughts. "I expect I'll marry him one day, Presti."

Knowing how they felt about each other, I was not surprised yet shocked all at once. "I thought we had agreed that marriage was a dead institution."

"Oh, yes, quite," Astrid replied earnestly. "Yet, I can't help imagining the felicity of becoming Mrs Astrid Bomalier-Brooke-Brooks."

"Something of a mouthful, Astrid."

"Isn't it?" She smiled, her face glowing in the dim aircraft lighting. Though I knew love had the power to destroy as much as offer utmost bliss, I wanted it for myself.

"Well, I shall be delighted to be your man of honour when the time comes."

"And I will be equally as pleased to be your best woman on your wedding day, Presti."

An indelicate snort burst from me at the thought. "I have no intention of marrying. I am content to remain Prestidigitation Jones for all time."

Astrid offered me one of her knowing smirks. "You will marry one day, Presti, and your husband will be the luckiest man on Earth."

I couldn't see it myself, but I liked the sound of Astrid's prediction too much for my own good.

Chapter Eight

WHAT HAD I done? I'd thought by brushing off Presti and never seeing him again, I'd forget all about him. How wrong I'd been.

I saw his soft smile when I closed my eyes at night. His striking eyes haunted my mind, and his gentle voice played on a constant loop in my head. I replayed the one night we'd spent in each other's company repeatedly, holding it in my memories with a death grip. I was terrified I might forget a single second of those few short hours I'd spent with a man who'd left an extraordinary impression on me.

I'd grown pathetic enough to pour over official photos taken that night for any images of Presti that might exist. His handsome features peered back at me from the photographs, his face caught in a deer-in-headlights expression as though thoroughly disbelieving his circumstances in that frozen moment.

Along with the official portrait, I'd managed to find him in several other shots. One caught him laughing with Astrid. Another captured his quizzical frown, and I found myself tormented with curiosity over what had perplexed him so. I wanted to give him answers to smooth the troubled lines between his eyes.

And, though the thought might be immature, Prestidigitation Jones was the hottest man I'd ever met.

"James? Can I come in?" George bellowed through my cracked open door.

Following my miserable treatment of Presti, I'd practically shut myself away, hiding in my rooms. At the same time, the fallout from being caught in Astrid and Presti's little protest rained down around me. Of course, the media had latched onto the possibility of something brewing between Astrid and me. She had given me a great hug after all. The possibility of a queer prince seemed inconceivable. Nobody suspected I'd been drawn to the man standing next to Astrid. Nobody questioned how long we'd held hands. As usual, the palace kept a dignified silence on the matter.

"Come in, George."

My brother, whom I had not seen since that night, looked deliriously happy. I suspected I knew the source of his joy. "I'm guessing I need to offer you some congratulations, George," I said as he bounced toward me.

George gripped me in a bear hug, lifted me off my feet, and twirled me about most un-regally. "She finally said yes," he cried.

Only then did I notice poor Harlan standing in the doorway looking as miserable as George looked joyful.

"Congratulations, George. You're a lucky man. I hope you strive to deserve her."

George flinched as if I'd struck him. "You don't think much of me, do you, James?"

"You're my brother, and I love you. We're just different people. I didn't mean to offend you, George."

George flicked a glance to Harlan before returning his steely gaze to mine. "I love Hannah more than anything, but I offered to walk away from her if that's what she wanted. Did you know that, James? And did you know that I've known forever that you're gay, but I've never said anything to anyone because I've been waiting — hoping — you'd come to me first? I'd hoped that you'd trust me enough to share that with me. Did you know that, James?"

"Christ," I mumbled. "I am sorry, George. I... I don't know what to say."

George shook his head. "Forget it. I know I can be a bit of a pill sometimes, but I'm not a complete arsehole, James. And I will always have your back."

My brother had struck me dumb several times in my life, but not like this. Not for a show of love toward me. "George..." I broke off, not knowing what to say.

"You liked that fellow. Didn't you?"

"Presti? I did. But I'm not... I'm not ready to come out yet."

George shrugged. "Then don't. But if you like him, James, don't let go of that."

"I've spent a handful of hours with him."

Again, George surprised me by laughing. "What did I say to you the day I met your sister, Harlan?"

I'd forgotten Harlan stood so quietly and solemnly at my door. If it had been anybody else, George and I would have been reckless to talk so openly in front of them. But Harlan was a vault; nothing he overheard would go any further. He didn't need money, and he didn't want fame.

"You said you could finally breathe because you'd found your missing piece." Harlan flushed, his eyes downcast as he spoke. His sister's marriage into my family would be a personal nightmare for Harlan—poor fellow.

"Wow. That was really…disgustingly sweet." I laughed, jumping out of George's reach as he playfully swatted at me.

"My point is, little brother, there is no set time frame for matters of the heart. I'm not saying you're in love with him, but if you like this guy, contact him at the very least. Talk to him. Find out if you could more than like him."

All I could do was nod and wonder who this man before me was and what he had done with my real brother.

"Anyway," George continued, "I came here to discuss the engagement announcement with you, not to pull your head out of your arse, though you were sorely in need of it."

"All right." I chuckled. "What do you need from me?"

"Just your support. Oh, and one hell of a bachelor party when the time comes." George winked while Harlan barked a laugh.

"Sure," I replied. "Whatever you want."

"The announcement is coming out tomorrow morning at eleven. Hannah will obviously be busy, so could you maybe…be somewhere with Harlan? If the press tracks him down, at least you'll be there to take the heat off him."

"I do not need to be babysat, George, as much as I appreciate it," Harlan muttered, the ever-present flush staining his cheeks.

"I promised Hannah I'd do whatever I had to do to make this easier for you, Harlan, and I meant it."

Harlan nodded. "Well, okay then. But you know James hates public life every bit as much as I do."

"Oh, I know, but James has years of practice. Besides, maybe you can talk some sense into him about this Prestidigitation chap." George smirked. I'd never seen him so happy, and he seemed set on making everyone just as joyful.

"We'll look out for each other," I added. "When will the big event be?"

"In the summer. Early June."

Eight months away. Not long at all. The press would be too busy with Royal Wedding fever to look too closely at my life. I figured I had an eight-month reprieve before I'd have to think about making my big public announcement.

"I am happy for you, George. Hannah will make a perfect queen."

George smiled, looking pleased with himself. My brother could often be boorish, prone to think too highly of himself, but I was happy for him. He clapped both me and Harlan on the shoulder and turned to leave. "I'll leave you two to figure out some plan for where you'll be tomorrow."

"We'll figure something out," I promised. "Congratulations again, George."

"Thanks." George stopped and turned to me once more. "And, James, I'd like it if you brought a date to my wedding…somebody you want to date." And with that, George winked and left me standing there with my mouth hanging open.

"Didn't expect that," Harlan said, breaking the silence

following George's departure.

"Not at all," I replied, my gaze still fixed on the door my brother had so casually walked through seconds ago after flooring me with his behaviour. Had I been too hard on George all this time?

"I shan't say anything about it," Harlan murmured. "About your sexuality, I mean."

I waved my hands about. "Pfft. I know that, Harlan. I trust you."

"Well, I should hope." Harlan smiled. "We are going to be family and all. And for what it's worth… I think Mr Jones would look quite dapper on your arm at the wedding of the century."

"Wedding of the century?" I laughed. "We're only twenty years into the century. Who knows what grand nuptials might occur in the remaining eighty."

Harlan nodded sagely. "Perhaps one with two grooms."

Harlan's words both thrilled and terrified me. "Perhaps," I murmured, utterly failing to conceal a tiny grin.

*

GEORGE'S ANNOUNCEMENT THE following day went off without a hitch. Harlan and I watched live coverage before we braved the great outdoors on the grounds of Balmoral. We'd helicoptered away from Buckingham Palace to a military airfield early this morning before switching to a small aircraft, arriving at the castle in Balmoral just in time to catch the exciting news.

Predictably, the media were going quite berserk. At first, I'd thought we'd overreacted by whisking Harlan away from the capital and the ensuing fanfare over the engagement, but the gaggle of press camped out at the palace gates when we'd arrived disabused me of that notion.

"Quite silly, isn't it?" Harlan said, his gaze shifting in the direction of the gates. "All this fuss because of a wedding."

"I asked my grandma once why they didn't abolish royalty now that we were nothing more than show ponies with no real power. She said we offered a distraction, a look into a fantasy. People still want to peer into the worlds of kings and queens, princes and princesses."

"Maybe that's all you are for some, James, but a lot of good is done too. Charity work. Focusing attention on causes." Harlan smiled almost sadly. "You aren't just show ponies."

"Will you be okay, Harlan? With all the attention."

Harlan shrugged. "It's not what I would have chosen for myself, but I want my sister to be happy. And George makes her happy."

"What about you? Your happiness." Darkening clouds rolled towards us, an early winter storm rolling in, the air already damp with fog and mist. I envisioned a perfect evening around the fire, with a good book and fine whiskey in hand while my brother lapped up the world's attention. I wasn't jealous, not of that, but I couldn't deny my envy of what he shared with Hannah.

"My happiness is simple, James. A quiet life. A home, a family. That's all I crave."

"Sounds wonderful."

"It could be yours too, James."

"I'm not destined for a quiet life…or a family of my own."

"Do you want it? That's what you must ask yourself. Forget destiny. Forget what you were born into. Decide what you want, and go after it."

We walked silently, lost to our thoughts, the dogs yapping and chasing squirrels.

"Do you think I can have what I want?" I asked. My life had been laid out for me since before I was born. Sure, I'd occasionally struggled against the plan, but mostly, I'd been content to ride the gentle stream. But what if I could fight the tide and get what I wanted?

"I don't see why not. It is the twenty-first century. Politically expedient, arranged marriages are no longer the norm for royalty."

"Yes, but what if… What if I wanted to marry a man?"

Harlan looked at me as if I'd asked him the most straightforward question ever asked. "I don't see how that's of concern to anybody but you and your groom."

If only that were so. I suspected a great many would have quite a bit to say about it, but ultimately, Harlan was right. I should be with someone I loved regardless of who they were.

"James," Harlan said, a severe frown creasing his forehead. "Take it from me. Life is short, over in the blink of an eye. Don't waste a second of it caring what everybody else wants for you."

Harlan and Hannah's parents had been killed three years ago, wiped out of existence when a lorry driver playing on his phone ran over the top of theirs and two other cars. Six innocent people and a pet dog died in the fireball. The lorry driver walked away with hardly a scratch.

"You're right, Harlan. And I have a letter to write."

We shared a smile before continuing on our stroll around the grounds. Letter writing was not the *done* thing anymore, but something whispered to me that Presti would enjoy corresponding in that method.

Predictably, we were informed on our return that the horde of reporters camped out at the gates of Balmoral were still there. Harlan and I remained safely ensconced behind the perimeter walls. Truthfully, we could stay here for months, but I knew I'd be wanted back in London soon so the world could see how happy and supportive I was of my brother's engagement. And I was. I just wished I didn't have to display it publicly.

When a fierce storm rolled in just as dusk fell, I sat alone in my room, pen and paper in hand. My desk faced the window, offering me a terrific view of the dark clouds occasionally split by bright lightning. Heavy rain thundered against the windowpanes, the distant trees whipping about in the ferocious gusts. I'd always loved storms. When caught in the middle of a tempest, a person knew they were alive as the wind and rain tore at them.

At least an hour had passed since we'd returned from our walk. I'd excused myself from Harlan and retreated to my room with the intention of writing a letter to Presti. My page remained pristinely white.

"Damn," I muttered to the empty room. "This shouldn't be so hard."

Yet it was. I hadn't treated Presti well at our parting. Maybe he'd hate receiving any sort of contact from me. Perhaps I should just pen an apology and be done with it. With him.

That thought made me sick and scared all mixed together.

Just write something, anything.

Two hours later, I'd written a six-page letter of mostly gibberish with an apology and an added splash of pleading for Presti to write back. I sealed and addressed the envelope using the address I'd been given by my father's onsite secretary before taking it to him for postage before I could change my mind.

The remainder of the night, I lay tossing and turning, wide awake and wondering how badly I'd messed things up and just how big of a fool I'd made of myself.

Chapter Nine

THE LAST TIME I'd received mail from abroad had been... Well, never. I did not receive mail. Nobody did. Text messages from Astrid, Mother, sometimes Larry, yes. Emails from work, university, some questionable business that assured me they could enhance my sex life, sure. But nobody sat down and wrote letters anymore. Not with pen and paper. How very odd.

This letter had also come from the palace. Of course, within the unopened, handwritten envelope might be nothing more than a printed copy of a standard thank you for attending the queen's festivities a little under two weeks ago.

Still, my shaking hands didn't get the memo. Why I felt nervous to open the missive confounded me. *Utterly ludicrous.* I tore it open, spoiling the expensive envelope entirely. Several pages fluttered to the floor about my feet.

Curious.

A thank you should take no more than one page—two at a stretch and with a gigantic font. Perhaps I had become embroiled in some sort of chain letter, whereupon I would need to send this on to at least six friends (four more than I possessed) or risk imminent ruin or death. As previously mentioned, I am somewhat prone to dramatics.

What I found upon retrieving the pages could not have shocked me more if the words leapt from the page and slapped me.

The letter was from Prince James. I discovered his signature on the second page I looked at. *Astounding*.

Once I collected the six pages—yes, six—I collapsed onto my bed as though my bones had de-solidified. What the dickens was this?

It took some time to order the pages correctly, but I was reading James's apologetic, charming, and entirely devastating letter before long. How was one to resist such an onslaught of charisma? His vulnerability quite beguiled me as he pleaded for me to forgive his behaviour and then humbly asked that I write back to him.

There was nothing to be done but call Astrid.

She answered after three torturous rings. "Presti, I saw you not one hour ago. Is everything okay? It is not like you to be so clingy."

"I've received a letter."

"A letter?"

"Mm."

"Handwritten?"

"Of course."

"And who penned the missive?"

"Prince James."

Astrid gasped. "Extraordinary."

"Mm."

"Well? What does he say?"

"This and that. Apologising for his behaviour when last we saw him. Asking me to write back."

"Write back?"

"Mm."

"Extraordinary."

"Quite."

"I shan't ask you to read it to me, Presti, what with privacy and all that, but was it splendid?"

"Naturally. The entire letter is peppered with snippets of James's personality so as to make it quite impossible for me to do anything other than dreamily admire him as a literal embodiment of a Prince Charming." I sounded ridiculous, but it was the truth.

"Remarkable. He did come across as one who could be quite an excellent belletrist. Do you plan to respond?"

"Well, I don't know. I can't seem to think straight. Shock and all. What do you think?"

"I think you must. It's manners to respond." I heard the flutters of excitement building in Astrid's tone.

Should I respond? "Of course." And then that heinous bitch, reality, gut punched me. "What the hell do I say?"

For a moment, Astrid said nothing, then she said, quite rapidly, "I'll be there in ten minutes. We'll need the best paper you have, a calligraphy pen, if possible. Far more romantic than a common ballpoint, candles and at least one bottle of wine. Oh, don't fuss about the paper; I have just the thing, but get the rest of the required accoutrements together. Larry will happily bring us sustenance, I'm certain. This looks set to be an all-nighter, Presti."

What the hell had I gotten myself into? Perhaps I should have kept this one little secret to myself. Too late now, Astrid was well and truly up to her naturally sculptured eyebrows in my and James's...penpalship?

True to her word, Astrid arrived in a swirl of excitement and zeal not ten minutes later. I listened as she almost incoherently babbled to my mother some excuse for her presence, which inexplicably seemed to involve the plight of sea otters being exploited on the internet for the viewing pleasure of the human population as they watched the otters frolicking in aquatic environments.

"Well," my mother said as she extricated herself from Astrid's enthusiasms at my bedroom door," let me know what I can do, as always." Mum smiled fondly and left us to it.

"Right," Astrid offered as soon as my door closed, "I've got parchment. Father ordered it online several years ago, but we never quite found a use for it. And now the perfect occasion presents itself. Oh, Presti, this is just marvellous."

"Mm."

Astrid froze and turned her seeking gaze to mine. "You seem enervated. Have you changed your mind? Do we need to rebuff the overtures of the prince?"

"It's not quite overtures, As. I think he's just lonely." Though we hadn't spent much time together and were, in fact, little better acquainted than strangers, I'd gotten the distinct impression that James not only would not have chosen his life but was positively lonely in it.

"Then be his friend, Presti. I can't imagine he has too many true ones, and he couldn't ask for a truer one than you."

"What if…I could see myself falling for someone like him. What if I do, and I end up getting hurt?"

"What if you don't? Matters of the heart are full of risks, but what is life without taking those risks to find the person made just for you?"

Part of me wanted to laugh at the absurdity of a prince of anywhere being made for me. But an image of James's vulnerable eyes, the phantom feel of his soft, warm lips on mine, overtook any hesitation I felt at replying to his letter.

"Okay. I shall become his pen pal but won't allow myself to think I will ever be anything more to him. I can't, Astrid. I must protect myself."

Astrid nodded. "Pen pals, then. Friends across the oceans and the pages."

"Yes. Yes, I can live with that."

"Let's begin, then."

"Let's. How?" I asked, still in something akin to shock at this turn in my life's fortunes.

"An acceptance of his apology to begin. And then follow his lead. Did he share himself with you? Or was it polite mentions of the weather and asking after your family?"

Though Astrid's eyes burned with curiosity, I knew she'd never ask to read the letter. But I could share titbits with her. Enough, at least, for her to guide me in this endeavour. She was, after all, the only one of us to ever have had a romance.

Three hours and almost two bottles of wine later, Astrid and I had achieved…nothing. Nothing but a growing pile of discarded pages filled with unsatisfactory words and sentiments. Too impersonal. Too cheesy. Too verbose. The list went on and on as to why we'd vetoed every attempt at return correspondence.

"We are wordsmiths, Presti," Astrid bemoaned. "Why can we not compose a suitable letter?" Astrid took a sip of yet another glass of wine.

She and I were not typically big consumers of alcohol, following some rather unfortunate incidents, but strange times called for strange behaviours.

"I expect it has something to do with Prince James's lips," I replied.

"His lips?"

"Mm."

Astrid's brows furrowed as she stared at me, seeking an explanation. "How so?"

"I can't seem to stop thinking about them. How glorious they felt pressed against my own—" Too late, I realised what I'd just blurted. At least I had my wine-addled brain to blame for my blabbermouth.

"Aha, I knew it," Astrid crowed. "I knew he kissed you. You came back with that same look of awe you had after Silkie introduced you to pornography."

"I had no idea that could go there and that—by all accounts—it would feel so good."

"I do not want to have this conversation again. I do think we've analysed that particular sex act to death. So, may we get back to Prince James and his luscious lips?" Astrid, astonishingly, waggled her eyebrows.

"Don't ever do that thing with your eyebrows again, As."

"Sorry. I blame the wine."

"I certainly hope so, and I never said his lips were luscious."

"But they were?"

"Oh yes, they were indeed. Like warm, soft pillows pressing against my own," I replied a little too dreamily for my liking. I had imbibed an awful amount of wine.

"That's not quite as erotic sounding as you think it is, Presti."

"It is."

"Hmm," Astrid murmured thoughtfully. "No. I stand by my original claim."

"Well!" I rather too aggressively shouted while reaching for my phone. "We'll see about that." I dialled.

"Who are you trying to call, Presti?" Astrid leaned against my side, trying to keep upright or see whose name was on my screen.

"I'm calling an adjudicator to—oh, hello. Yes. James. Sorry to trouble you and all, but I was hoping you could settle a matter between Astrid and myself."

"Presti?" James asked, sounding adorably perplexed.

"Yes. Yes, it is Presti. Now, I ask you, James, do you not think it is somewhat erotic to describe lips as soft, warm pillows?"

Silence.

"James?"

"Yes. I'm still here. I'm just not sure what's happening."

"You're adjudicating a disagreement between Astrid and myself. I think I should put you on speaker. Let me put you on speaker. Astrid should be able to hear your chrysostomatical voice when you agree with me about the eroticism of your lips." I fumbled about, searching for how one utilised the speaker function on my phone. Astrid remained still at my side, unhelpfully gaping at me.

Finally, I managed the feat. "Right," I said with utter confidence in my chosen course of action. "Now, James, do you not find it quite erotic that I described your lips as soft, warm pillows when we… Well, I shouldn't say it over the airwaves. Anybody might be listening in, unless, of course, you've likely got some measures in place to prevent eavesdropping. Wonderful spy stuff. But do you agree with me? You, James, not Astrid, because she does not."

"Have you been drinking?" James asked.

"I have, but my sobriety is not the issue here. Choose a side, James."

James chuckled before offering an answer. "I find it adorable that you think that of my lips."

"But adorable is not erotic," I replied.

"How diplomatic," Astrid gushed. "Isn't he diplomatic, Presti? You are quite right about his chrysostomatical voice. He might easily be a voiceover man if he weren't a prince."

"Adorable is okay, I guess," I continued somewhat sullenly, "but I was aiming for something a little more erotic."

"Dare I ask what is going on over there?" Prince James asked, sounding more perfect than any mortal should.

"I received your letter."

"And it warranted alcohol and a discussion over how to describe my lips."

"It was unexpected," I replied.

"I wanted to apologise and also," James said, his voice

dipping into a whisper, "I didn't want to say goodbye to you."

"Yes, Mrs Jones," Astrid yelled, "I can help you polish the silverware. One never does know who might show up for dinner." Astrid fled my room with a wink and a slight wobble on her unsteady feet.

"That was subtle." James laughed.

"We don't have silverware," I replied, feeling quite tongue-tied over the developing events.

"You are wonderful, Presti."

"Are you certain you have the right person?" I asked, convinced James thought he was conversing with some other Presti. I really must add wine to my list of banned consumables.

"I only know one Prestidigitation, and he is quite wonderful."

"I did like your lips," I exclaimed.

"I'm glad. I liked kissing you too."

"I've been trying to reply to your letter, but, well, I can't express what I want to express. Words are failing me," I sighed, frustrated by my lack of skill with the written word. "I guess I'm not sure I'm doing it right. Letter writing, that is. And then I began fearing you might suffer from epistolophobia, but of course, if you had a fear of receiving correspondence, you would not have asked me to write back even if I do it wrong."

"There is no right or wrong way. Just write…whatever is on your mind. Whatever you wish to share with me."

Huh. Indeed, I could do that. "Even if it's to complain about that uncomfortable feeling of wearing new underwear?"

James barked a laugh, a sound I wanted to hear more of. "Yes, even if it's that. I don't have many friends, Presti, and I greatly enjoyed your company. I want to be your friend."

"I would like that too."

"Well, it's settled then. We're friends," James declared.

"Pen pals," I agreed. "And as your friend, may I congratulate your family on your brother's upcoming nuptials? The media here is quite gaga over it all."

"And here," James sighed. "Listen, Presti, I'd love to stay and talk with you, but I'm afraid you did call me at a somewhat awkward time. I'm in the middle of a public engagement."

"Right. Sorry. Time differences and all that. It isn't the middle of the night over there."

"Nope. And I'm about to step out into the opening of a youth centre. But promise me you'll write. Anything at all, Presti. Just write me."

There was that thread of vulnerability in James, the one that tugged mightily on my heartstrings. "Well, it wouldn't be much of a penpalship if I didn't write you. So, I promise," I vowed. "Take care, James."

"And you," James replied. And then he was gone.

Before Astrid returned to my room three-quarters of an hour later, I'd penned seven pages of utter nonsense to Prince James of England, thus beginning our penpalship.

Chapter Ten

LESS THAN A week after the delightfully drunken phone call from Presti, his letter arrived. The envelope — addressed in what I could only assume to be Presti's chicken-scratch writing — remained clenched, unopened, in my hand. My personal secretary, Scott, had handed it to me on my way to a family meeting to discuss George and Hannah's wedding.

Both of my parents somehow managed to make time in their hectic schedules. Mother, especially, had taken the matrimonial bull by the horns, steering every detail of the event toward her wishes. George didn't seem to care at all about the ceremony, or so he announced. Hannah's only stipulation thus far was for complete autonomy over her dress. Since Hannah was an incredibly stylish woman, I couldn't see this being a problem.

Even as I listened to discussions about guest lists, bridal parties, colours, and flowers, Presti's letter burned my fingers. I itched to flee the room, rip open the envelope and devour the con-tents. Had he written it that same night he'd called? Would it be full of the drunken ramblings of Prestidigitation Jones? I couldn't wait to find out.

"Do sit still, James," my mother admonished, though she smiled. "What is in that envelope that has you ready to burst out of your skin?"

Shrugging as nonchalantly as possible, I said, "I don't know. I haven't opened it yet."

"Is it from your young man?" my father asked. I'd already told him of the letter I'd sent to Presti. Where I'd been expecting admonishment, I'd received only gentle support.

"I think so."

My parents shared a glance, having one of those wordless conversations couples who've been together years seemed to manage.

"Perhaps we might take a short break. Twenty minutes, I think?" Mum suggested.

"Thirty," I answered as I leapt from my seat.

My father's office, where we'd been meeting, was at the far end of the same floor where my rooms were. Years had passed since I last ran these corridors, but I flew down them now, draw-ing the frowns of a handful of staff. This entire level contained only private residences and offices of my immediate family. Though beautifully furnished, there was nothing of great value or historical importance here, unlike in the public areas.

For all my complaining about my life, I knew how lucky I was. I was happy to serve and do my duty, even enjoying most of my charity work. I just wished I could do it privately, without all the media attention and huge crowds.

Slamming my door shut, I threw myself on my bed and tore the envelope open. Presti's nearly illegible writing glared back at me, all seven pages. I couldn't read it fast enough.

His words, some serious, others filled with light-heartedness, were like a balm to my soul. He told me of his studies, hours spent in the garden alone or with his mother, days spent with Astrid, a rather odd conversation he'd had with a Silkie Bellbird. Presti's life seemed like a rainbow, colourful and rich.

As I read Presti's letter for the second time, I realised these pages were an escape. I found somewhere special among the spaces between the messily scratched letters — where I could just be me.

Between our shared words, we'd created a world, a place for the two of us where no one else was welcome. Where none could find us. On these pages, I wouldn't be told to stand straighter, speak more clearly, or show more interest. Between Presti and me, there existed only…us.

As much as I wanted to write back immediately, I knew my parents would come looking for me — or rather, send someone to find me — if I didn't return after my half-hour reprieve.

Tucking the letter in my pocket, I returned to my father's office feeling lighter than when I'd left it.

"Well," my mother said as soon as I walked in," I guess it's safe to say the letter was from your young man."

"He's not mine. Presti and I are friends, but yes, it was from him."

"I don't kiss my friends in the manner Dad caught you two," George added. For his trouble, Hannah slapped his forearm.

"Ignore him," Hannah said. "I'm so pleased you have another friend, James. I know it's hard for you. You're so like Harlan, and you are both such wonderful men. I have hope you'll both find the happiness you deserve."

"Thank you, Hannah," I replied, squeezing her wrist.

"Oh, gag," George said. "The fam already loves you, Han. No need to kiss their arses."

"You are a total pill, George."

"Yeah, but you love me." George made obnoxious kissy noises as he batted his lashes at Hannah. The entire scene made me equal parts nauseous and jealous.

"I wouldn't be here if I didn't. Poor Harlan is quite beside himself now that I've asked him to walk me down the aisle."

"You know Arthur will do it if that makes things easier for Harlan?" my mother offered. Who would walk Hannah down the aisle had been one of the first points agreed upon about this wedding. With her father so tragically killed, her brother seemed the obvious choice. I wondered how Harlan would manage the feat, though I knew he'd do it for his sister.

"Thank you, Miriam, but I want it to be Harlan, and he's quite determined."

"Very well, but just know that Arthur can step in if needed." Mum smiled warmly at Hannah. George hadn't been lying when he said we all loved Hannah. "Now, on to the wedding party. Besides James, is there anyone else you'd like to stand with you, George?"

"James will do just fine." George winked at me. Since his engagement, he'd become both more relaxed and mature. Perhaps all this time he'd just been searching for happiness, and now he'd found it, he was like a new man.

Would that be me one day? Could I come out to the world if it meant chasing that happiness? For the first time, I believed I could. Especially now that my family knew, and they still loved me.

"You okay, James?" my mother asked.

"Thank you," I exclaimed. "I'm ashamed to admit that I thought you all might have turned your backs on me when you found out, but you've been nothing but supportive. About me being queer, I mean."

"And we'll continue to be supportive, whether you eventually come out or not," my father said. "Whatever you decide, James, we'll have your back."

Swallowing the lump in my throat, I steered the conversation back to the far safer topic of the wedding. "So, um… Morning suit or tuxes?"

Several hours later, I left Dad's office, my ears bleeding from listening to the minutiae of what wedding flowers meant and why a caramel mud cake was not an appropriate choice. Poor George nodded off at one stage, receiving Hannah's elbow to the ribs for his trouble.

If George's engagement had taught me one thing, it was that I didn't see a wedding in my future. I mean, theirs would be a traditional wedding, and the fuss and media attention was already making me ill. The chaos and pandemonium that would explode following the announcement of my engagement to another man would be nothing short of epic. And it would be far more than I could handle.

Though I might not want the wedding, I did want the

marriage—or at least a committed relationship. I wanted a partner. Was I asking too much? I hoped not.

The other thing I'd learned from George's engagement was how tiring wedding planning could be. My eyes slid shut as I ate the small meal that had been prepared and sent to my room. I sipped my tea, hoping to stay awake enough to start another letter to Presti.

As I thought about what I wanted to say, I realised I had so much I wanted to tell him about. Wedding plans, upcoming charity events, especially any involving animals or the environment, the jubilee party coming up in a few weeks, the David Attenborough biography I was halfway through, the text I'd ordered about ethnobotany that I planned to read next, my surprise at how supportive my family had been, and my shame that I was so surprised. All this and more I itched to scribble down to share with Presti.

All my life, I'd kept myself shut away from others, afraid to let them in, let them see me. With Presti, I didn't feel that fear. Watching him be so unapologetically himself had been liberating and emboldening. For the first time, I felt brave enough to show the real me to another human being.

So, I wrote to Presti about how I hated the twitch in Simon de Montfort's left eye when he felt exasperated by my indifference to his plans. I wrote how my favourite spot in the world was a small grove of trees on the banks of a small creek running through Gran's estates in Balmoral. I explained in minute detail my fascination with great white sharks and my secret love/hate relationship with the movie *Jaws*. I told him I loved tomato sauce but hated tomatoes and drank tea with no milk but never coffee.

My letter was pages long, probably way more than Presti would be interested in reading. But I felt courageous enough to try, to see if Presti might like James Wales the man, not my title or wealth. And maybe if he didn't, then that was okay, too.

*

ALMOST TWO WEEKS had passed since I'd sent my response, and no letter from Presti arrived — twelve torturous days where my imagination ran amok in leaps and bounds. In one particularly dire early morning nightmare, I imagined Presti selling my letters to the press. I'd thought that was the worst thing that could happen. Yet, when I imagined Presti bored or disgusted by the glimpses I'd given him of my true self, a thick, deep sadness almost drowned me. Or perhaps he had convinced himself I had a phobia of receiving letters.

Why did I care so much? Why this man? Why now? These were questions I had no answers for, at least none I was willing to admit. I didn't want to think about what it all meant or why I was so willing to put myself out there for Presti. I could not allow myself to wonder if I'd met somebody whom I wanted to become important to me. Somebody I might be willing to come out for. The repercussions of letting Presti into my life terrified me.

Yet I couldn't stop.

I couldn't stop thinking about Presti. His wide-eyed innocence, joy for life, and complete disregard for what others might think of him. His complete willingness to just be him. An ongoing, nagging thought scratched away at me constantly. Could I be as free to be myself as Presti was? Could I do that if the reward was freedom from my regal persona and having Presti in my life? Or that I allowed myself to have someone special in my life.

These were ridiculous thoughts. Everything was stacked against us. We lived in two different worlds, two different countries. Presti showed himself to the world while I cowered behind a crown. He was gorgeous, and I was…not.

Ugh, I was so sick of myself. Tired of my constant thoughts about Presti and my attempts at friendship with a man so different from me that he might as well have come from Mars.

It was past time to distract myself with something else. Something that wouldn't drag me into a self-indulgent existential crisis. I needed a timeout—space from…well, from my life. I needed to make a call.

"James?"

"Yeah, it's me. Are you busy?"

"At two in the morning? I'm busy sleeping." Harlan punctuated his words with a garbled yawn.

Jesus, I'd been so caught up in my head that I hadn't even realised the time when I'd dialled Harlan's number. "I'm so sorry, I didn't realise the time. I'll call you back tomorrow."

"Well, I'm awake now. What's so urgent you couldn't wait till sunup to call?"

"I've got a charity event in Paris the day after next. I was hoping you might like to come along?"

Silence.

"Harlan?"

"As your…date?"

"Christ, no. Sorry, Harlan, I meant just to Paris. We could go out a bit, see the sights."

"Um. Sure, I guess." Harlan yawned loudly again. "Are you

all right, James?"

Was I? I didn't know, and that was half the problem. "I need some time away. Away from duty and all that being a public figure business, but I don't want to be alone. I don't want to think."

"Got it." Harlan's voice held a smile as if he knew exactly what I was talking about. "A distraction, then."

"Exactly."

"Very well. I'm not certain you've chosen the right person for the job, but I'll do my best."

"Thank you. I'll make all the arrangements. You just have to show up."

Harlan chuckled, his laughter broken by another yawn. "That I can do. Now, if I could just get back to sleep…"

"Of course. Sorry again for the late hour."

"Goodnight, James."

"Night, Harlan." I hung up feeling decidedly more upbeat than when I'd called.

Though I did not know what Harlan and I would get up to in Paris, an idea began to take shape — the time for me to embrace my sexuality had arrived. A visit to one of Paris's many fine gay bars seemed just the place to dip my toe in.

Chapter Eleven

ASTRID CAME BARRELLING toward me, clearly out of breath and clutching her pearls—had she been wearing them. A livid red painted her face, and her chest heaved as if she were some damsel in distress. I'd never seen her quite so agitated nor so…athletic.

"There you are, Presti. Your mother said you'd be home soon, but I simply could not wait." Astrid panted, resting her hands on her knees as she sucked in large gulps of air.

"What on earth is wrong?" I cried, fearing something dreadful had to have occurred to inspire such physical activity in one usually so keen to avoid running of any kind. "You don't run, Astrid."

"I am perfectly aware," she gasped, still reeling in huge breaths. "It's James."

"James?"

"Yes. He's been… Well, he was…"

"Oh, do spit it out, Astrid. Is he well?"

"Perfectly healthy, but I'm afraid he's become embroiled in something of a scandal," Astrid gasped, thrusting her phone in my face.

An image of a shirtless James sandwiched between two men in a smoky, dimly lit room accosted my vision. Putting aside the scandalous nature of the photograph, semi-naked James looked positively dreamy.

"What happened?" I murmured, unable to draw my gaze from the bare-chested prince with the serene expression on his face and an obvious erection in his nether regions.

"Seems he was snapped in the appropriately named Cox gay bar in Paris. Clearly, this was well into his night out. One can only imagine he was attempting to go incognito — there's a definite hint of an unnatural moustache, and earlier photographs have him in a shirt and baseball cap."

"Poor James," I muttered, still unable to look away from his blindingly beautiful bare torso.

"Quite. The palace is offering a blanket 'no comment', but 'friends 'are already being quoted as 'knowing there was something different 'about James. This will turn into quite the hubble show, I suspect."

"Mm."

"Well?" Astrid asked, a gentle annoyance in her tone. "Are you going to do something about it?"

"Me?"

"You. Presti, that boy is lonely, with limited friends. He has extended the hand of friendship to you. I should think he may wish to hear from you now. He may need to know he has your support."

"Do you think that's the best course of action?"

"It is the only course," Astrid adamantly replied.

"You are quite right." Poor James must be suffering under the burden of his unfortunate outing. He'd asked me to be his friend. How could I not be? Friendship, I was good at.

"Let's get indoors; this is not a conversation that should be overheard," I said, already moving toward my home. "You can tell me everything you know on our way."

"I know very little," Astrid began, falling into step at my side. "Larry called me and sent me that photo. From what I can gather, it is all speculation, but the photo speaks a thousand words. It appears Harlan—Earl of Fenwick—was also present, though he seems to have escaped infamy."

"Poor James."

"So you've said."

"He must be mortified."

"Well, of course," Astrid snorted. "Imagine having this splashed all over the world. No privacy. No control over your own story. Horrifying."

We made it home with no further words passing between us, to be greeted by my concerned-looking mother.

"Ah, I might have filled her in…on you and James," Astrid explained. "Not the… Well, not everything, just the penpalship."

"We're sticking with that, then? Penpalship."

"I think we must," Astrid replied.

"Oh, Presti," Mum said as we passed the threshold. "How awful. The paparazzi are such vermin."

"Mm."

"How do you think poor James will cope?"

"I recall a great and terrible vulnerability in the shade of his eyes, in the tone of his words. James wants nothing more than a private life, not this…this terrible invasion. I think he will be mortified. How does one help him with that?"

"By being a friend. By giving him what he asked of you. Friendship," my mother replied kindly. Penelope Jones may not be a great intellect, but she knew people. She understood them in a way most of us don't. It was one of the many things that made her so remarkable.

"I can do that," I murmured.

"Of course you can," Astrid assured me. "You are a wonderful friend, Presti. The best."

Nodding, I excused myself and made for the privacy of my room. James's privacy had been invaded quite enough already. I didn't intend to stomp over it again by having my mother and Astrid listen to our conversation.

As it turned out, I needn't have worried. He did not answer my call, nor any of the other many (I refuse to confirm a number) I made over the next thirty-six hours. Prince James of England had gone dark. He had not been spotted out and about; his family refused to divulge his location or discuss him in any way.

The only official comment on the scandal came from Harlan, who'd issued a statement telling the world that the night out had been his idea, the venue his choice. Speculation about the sexuality of the future king's future brother-in-law became a hot topic, yet it wasn't quite enough to completely shift the spotlight off James.

My mind had been able to think of little else but James. I'd wanted to be his friend through all this, but he'd rejected me. He wouldn't answer a single one of my calls. I'd left no messages when my calls went unanswered. I didn't know what to say. And paranoia that somebody may eavesdrop on my calls stilled my tongue. How did James live like this? So exposed and vulnerable.

All these thoughts shuffled through my mind as Astrid, Larry, and I sullenly walked to Pawn Stars to walk my mother home after work on an ordinary Tuesday evening. Astrid had scarcely left my side since the scandal broke. Naturally, this resulted in Larry's presence on my other side.

"I am certain you two could find far more interesting amusements than walking Mum and me home," I tried again.

"Prestidigitation Jones. We will not go over this again. I am your rock, your stoic and able helpmate in times of crisis. I will not abandon my post," Astrid replied.

"Astrid will not leave you, Presti, and I will not leave Astrid. Make your peace with it," Larry added.

"We are not at bloody war," I replied, smiling. "I'm really quite all right."

"Nonsense. You have that unfortunate crease you get in your forehead whenever you fret over something."

Automatically, my fingers went in search of this crease. Perhaps if I managed to smooth it out, I might get a moment's peace.

The crease was still there five minutes later when we arrived at Pawn Stars to be greeted by my mother, who told me she wished she could ease my troubles as she kissed my apparently craterous forehead.

"I am quite okay," I tried yet again.

"Non—"

"Nonsense," I sighed. "Yes, I know. You've all made it quite clear you think me on the verge of some kind of breakdown. James did not reply to my letter, nor did he answer my calls earlier. James does not wish my friendship, so it is not my place to agonise over his current circumstances."

"Yes, but that's not you, Presti," my mother said. "Once you care for someone, you're in it for life."

I did care about James, and Mum was right: I wasn't the sort to easily switch that off. Friendship with me might be bloody hard to come by but even harder to lose. James didn't need me though. Why that realisation should be a surprise was quite beyond me. We were two very disparate people from very dissimilar worlds.

"So, what's the plan for tonight? Board games? Charades? What have you planned for me tonight to keep my mind from vespering back to merry old England?" Last night, my fate had been to endure a marathon of *Schitt's Creek* — a show I loved. However, it is not much fun when one is forced to watch it sandwiched between a best friend and her paramour.

"Well," Mum began as she started locking up Pawn Stars. "I thought we'd do something of a bake-off. Howard is bringing everything we need to bake enough sweet treats to make us all sick to our stomachs."

"Um…great? Perhaps we could ration what we eat and take the leftovers to Mrs Nichols for her homeless shelter. Or is that too Marie Antoinette? Let them eat cake and all," I said.

"I believe that quotation has been debunked," Larry replied.

"Really? Huh. Where does that leave us with the sweet treats and the homeless?"

"I'm certain Mrs Nichols will appreciate anything. We shall

have a wonderful evening baking. It is very therapeutic, after all." Astrid linked her arm in mine as we walked.

"And," Larry added, "we can call it the Marie-never-said-that bake-athon." He was turning out to be quite an asset to our little group. Fit right in, as the saying went.

For a while, we walked quietly, each of us comfortable with the silence.

"How was your day, Mum?" I asked eventually.

"Wonderful. Ellery McWilliams came in, claiming she wanted to pawn a 1940s dinner set. However, I am sure she was only there to see Mr Foster. Something is brewing there, I can tell. Unfortunately for Ellery, Mr Foster was at his other branch. Something about a possible embezzler over there." Mum breathed and continued, "Apparently, the till was out by seventeen dollars just last week alone."

"Terrible," I replied, trying to keep my thoughts in the moment and not wandering back to James and his troubles.

"Is that Howard sitting against your front door?" Larry asked.

"Certainly not…unless he's lost his key again."

The last of the afternoon sun cast a glare on the figure slouched against our door. The magnificent bougainvillea, which we'd only recently agreed upon the colour of its flowers being aubergine, blocked a good portion of our visitor. Long legs clad in denim poked out, a pale, nicely muscled arm rested against his side. But the face remained hidden.

Tiny footsteps of nerves pitter-pattered up and down my spine. It wasn't fear making my circuits haywire but more a sensation or feeling that we were on the precipice of a momentous moment in our lives. Something big barrelled toward me even as I wondered who on earth had set up home on my mother's front porch. Surely it couldn't be who I thought?

"Oh my god," Astrid whispered. "Oh my god. Presti, this is momentous."

What on earth?

And then I watched as my mother effected a low bow. "Your Highness."

What?

"What?" I shouted, shocked and surprised, pitching my voice too loud.

"Please don't curtsey, Ms Jones," James said as he struggled to his feet.

"What!" I shouted again.

"I hope it's okay that I've just turned up on your doorstep," James mumbled, his gaze fixed on mine. "I needed to get away and… Well, Kincumber seemed as good a place as any."

"What!"

"Do stop shouting, Presti," Astrid said before turning her attention back to the prince and continuing, "I think perhaps he is broken, James."

"I am not broken," I sniffed. "Shocked. Perplexed. Bamboozled. But not broken."

"Then, for goodness sake, find your manners and invite His Highness inside," Mum added as she opened our front door.

"May I?" James asked when I remained still and silent.

"Of course." I gestured for James to precede me into the bowels of our small, decidedly un-palace-like residence.

We marched, all five of us, single file down the long hallway past bedrooms and bathrooms to spit us out in our comfortable living room.

Things did not get less awkward as we stood around, shifting uncomfortably as we wrestled with how to behave under these extraordinary circumstances. Could I be dreaming? No other valid explanation for this strange turn of events seemed plausible.

"Um," James bravely began, "I don't believe we've met." He extended his hand toward Larry.

"Lawrence Brooke-Brooks, Your Honour." Larry shook the prince's hand and nodded. *Your Honour. Dear god.*

Prince James smiled that blinding smile. "It's just James. And it's lovely to meet you, Lawrence."

"Larry."

"Larry," James agreed. "I guess you are all shocked to see me here."

"Well," my mother said, gently patting James's shoulder. "We have seen the news…terribly invasive."

"Absolute monsters plastering those photographs all over. Abhorrent," Astrid said.

"Appalling invasion of privacy," Larry added.

Then, all eyes turned to me, doubtless waiting for me to add my outrage to the consensus. I remained silent—mute, like a stunned mullet. My brain could not make sense of Prince James standing so casually in my mother's living room, draped in an ordinary T-shirt and jeans ensemble.

The world as I knew it had tipped upside down, turned inside out. What was I supposed to do with a prince of England in my home?

"Presti?" Prince James said. "You seem...unusually quiet."

"Isn't he?" Astrid agreed. "Usually, when Presti is thrown for a loop, he becomes positively loquacious. Verbally vomits out every thought in his head. This silence is most odd."

"May I speak to James alone?" I'd hardly got my request out when I saw the retreating backs of the three people I loved most in the world. They fled as if hell's hounds were on their tails, nipping at their heels, leaving me quite alone with James and with not a clue what to say to him.

For a moment, we stared at each other. Then I stepped forward, opened my arms and pulled him into a hug. His larger body fit nicely against mine, his muscles trembling until he finally relaxed a little.

"Presti," he whispered, his breath ruffling my hair. "I..."

"Sh," I murmured. "Sh. It's all right now. I have you. You're safe here."

James's body slumped even further into my hold, his tenseness easing—this poor, lonely man. My heart ached for him.

"How do you feel?" I asked, my arms still tight around his body.

"I feel a little nauseous. And I can't seem to stop shaking."

"That's not... I meant, how are you feeling about what's happened to you?"

James carefully extricated himself, taking a few steps away from me but maintaining eye contact. The teal of his eyes appeared darker, stormier than I remembered. His mouth turned down into an ill-suited frown. If ever a set of lips were made for smiling, they were James's.

"I ran away," he muttered. "Harlan offered... He tried to

take the fall for the entire debacle, and I let him. And I ran."

"James—"

"No. I am a coward, Presti." James tugged on the strands of his messy hair. I couldn't be sure if he did so in frustration or as an act of self-flagellation—punishment for his perceived cowardice.

"Have you spoken to Harlan?"

"Several times." James lowered his eyes, hardly daring to glance at me. "I don't even know what I'm doing here. I had planned to come out, but then it happened…that night out and those pictures. I lost my nerve because I didn't want it to be like that. I wanted to come out without much fuss, but then my…obvious pleasure at being sandwiched between two men was plastered all over the world. All I could think was how safe you made me feel and I…" James shook his head, seeming to run out of steam.

Instinct drove me as I opened my arms for him again. James didn't hesitate, settling into my embrace as if it was the only place he wanted to be on earth. He felt so right nestled against me.

"I'm so sorry, James," I crooned as I held him. "So sorry. Nobody should be outed in that fashion."

"I haven't even spoken to my parents." James's voice was muffled against my throat. "They must be horribly disappointed."

"Because you're gay?" I asked, my blood beginning to simmer.

"No. Because of those photos."

"They're not… I mean, the royal family aren't homophobic?"

"Not horribly, no. My parents and brother have been great.

But the rest of the family… Well, there's more of a quiet homophobia. Something along the lines of 'It'd be so much easier if you were not queer, James'."

"I see."

We were still draped about each other, and though conversing in this manner was somewhat awkward, I had no desire to untangle myself from James. And he was quite welcome to remain in my embrace for as long as it benefited his equilibrium.

"Ah, something of an awkward question, James."

"Mm-hmm"

"Does *anyone* know you're here?"

"Not a soul."

"Okay. Follow-up question. How much trouble might I be in for offering sanctuary to a prince?"

James laughed, a wondrous sound. "Is that an invite for me to stay?"

"It is," I replied. "Do you accept?"

"Wholeheartedly."

There was so much to do. Advise Mum James would be staying. Stock up on meals that are more fit for the royal palette. Purchase sheets with a thread count higher than ten. Put out the three-ply toilet paper. Swear Astrid to silence and best behaviour.

All that could wait.

Because James was still in my arms, and I liked it far too much for it to be over just yet.

Chapter Twelve

PENELOPE JONES AND her son made me feel more welcome in their small two-bedroom cottage than I had ever felt in the great rooms and halls of palaces and castles. While Penelope set about cleaning an already spotless home, Presti set about "regalising" their abode. Astrid and Larry were charged with purchasing necessary supplies. Whatever they were.

Try as I might to help, Penelope placed me on her couch and ordered me not to move an inch. I was to rest and recover from my jetlag. Though they whispered amongst themselves in another room, I heard the panic as they discussed how to host a royal guest. Adorable seemed to be the most appropriate word to describe every one of them.

Twenty minutes ago, I'd sent a text to my father. I had not divulged my location, but I'd promised him I was okay and asked him to give me a few days to figure things out. His reply had been typically brief, simply asking me to call him when I felt up to it. Deep down, I suspected him to be panicking over my disappearance. I hoped Billy and Gordon wouldn't be in trouble over this.

They weren't supposed to let me out of their sight once I left the palace or wherever I was staying at the time, but I hadn't let them know I was leaving. I'd snuck out like a thief in the night and made my way to the airport with Harlan's help, then onto a commercial flight to Sydney using my *ordinary* passport. Most people had no idea the surname of the royal family — my family. If I'd held a gun to their heads, ordinary people wouldn't know who James Wales was.

Presti's question from earlier rattled about in my mind, unwilling to give me a moment's peace. How did I feel? My life, my great secret, had been blown apart, scattered about in a handful of images for the entire world to see — those photos. My god, if you looked closely enough — and people had — it was clear enough to see I'd been hard while dancing, sandwiched between those two men. My obvious erection had been the topic of conversation on several news panels, the butt of constant jokes and the evidence for some of my debauched and shameful life.

Spasms of horror and nausea rocked me as I sat on Ms Jones's faux suede couch. I bent forward, put my head between my knees and prayed for the last three days to have been a nightmare.

"James?"

Jumping at the call of my name, I saw Presti standing over me with several rolls of toilet paper in his hand. His lovely eyes watched me closely as if expecting me to fall apart at any second. Perhaps I would.

"The entire world saw my hard-on," I blurted.

Presti nodded sagely. "Mm. They did rather, though if we were to look for the silver lining, it was fairly impressive."

"Thanks," I snorted. "I feel so…lost, Presti. I don't know what to do or how to fix this."

Presti put the toilet paper on the coffee table and sat beside me. "Do you want to fix it? What I mean is, do you want to tell the world you're not gay, and that photo was nothing more than a drunken night out?"

"No. Maybe. I don't know. It'd be easier."

"For whom? A bunch of people you don't know? People who can't stand the thought of you being anything other than a straight white man? It would certainly be easier for them. Maybe it'd be easier for you in the short term."

"People will hate me. A large—too large—part of the population will hate me."

"Sure. For the few seconds a day, week, or month when they'll even think of you. But if you deny who you are because of them, that's a pain you'll live with every second of every day of every week for the rest of your life."

Beautiful and wise. Prestidigitation Jones was a deadly combination of extraordinary, and he was doing nothing to extinguish my crush on him.

"My mother has always told me," Presti continued, "that we must each march to the beat of our own drum. We can't match the beat of any other, and if we try, we're doomed to an awkward, uncomfortable, and miserable existence."

"That may be true of most, but I'm a prince. I have duty and responsibility."

"People always blamed Winnie Frankston for the king abdicating. They said he loved her so much he gave up the throne for her. But I think he loved himself enough to give himself a shot at a life he wanted, a future he could live with. Now—" Presti smirked. "—I'm not suggesting you run off with an American divorcee with fabulous style, but perhaps you could love yourself enough to let yourself have the life you want. Not the life a bunch of courtiers and strangers who take entirely too much interest in a life that is not theirs want for you."

"Would it be terribly needy of me to ask for another of your amazing hugs?"

Presti smiled. "Not at all," he murmured, pulling me close and holding me again.

"Um, sorry to interrupt, but just a quick question," Penelope Jones said softly.

Rather than pull away from me completely, Presti made a rather wonderful manoeuvre that managed to leave me tucked into his side, one arm still around my shoulders. Though I was bigger than him, I felt enveloped by him. Ms Jones looked at us with a kind of wonder in her expression.

"What's up, Mum?"

"Well." Penelope wrung her hands, her eyes flicking between Presti and me. "Let's just barrel right through this potential awkwardness… I was wondering about the sleeping arrangements. If separate beds are required, I can stay at Howard's."

"No. No, I do not want to put anyone out," I said, horrified I might be kicking this wonderful woman out of her home.

"Nonsense. Howard will be thrilled."

"Mum and Howard haven't agreed to cohabit yet, but they

do spend an awful lot of nights together," Presti added.

Did he want his mother to go so I had my own bed? Of course, he did. We'd shared one kiss, spoken a few words, and exchanged a small handful of letters, and he hadn't replied to the last I'd sent. Whether or not we shared a bed at this stage of our relationship shouldn't even be a question. I'd have jumped at the chance to sleep with Presti, but it shouldn't even be on our radar.

"I am sorry. I didn't mean to force anyone from their own bed," I muttered. " I could sleep on the couch."

Presti and Penelope gaped at me as if I'd grown a second head. "No guest of mine sleeps on the couch. And that," Penelope said, "has nothing at all to do with your royalness."

"Thank you," I managed to squeak out. I'd heard the term salt of the earth bandied about many times, but here they were, two of the finest examples I could hope for. One held me tight against him as if he knew how close I was to shattering apart, the other standing protectively over us as if quite prepared to throw herself on a grenade for us if needed.

"Well, that's settled," Penelope said, starting to turn away. She stopped and looked back at us. "Just so you know, if you wanted to share a bed, that's quite okay with me. Presti is an adult, after all, and he no longer needs me to protect his virtue."

A line of heat shot up Presti's throat, his skin colouring a livid pink. "Thank you, Mother," he squeaked.

"Not that he has no virtue left," Penelope ran on. "I mean, unless I missed it, he's still a virgin."

"Oh god," Presti moaned, pushing his forehead into my chest.

"Not that I expect to be alerted to his deflowering, but a

mother always feels as if she'd just know when momentous moments occur in her children's lives."

Presti groaned and readjusted himself, so now his face pressed into my neck. I kissed the top of his head without a second thought. "Um. If it makes you feel any better, Ms Jones, I'm no kind of Lothario myself."

"Well, I must say that is good to hear. The press does tend to make you out as a rabid fornicator."

"Mother!" Presti yelled.

"Sorry. I did want to be quite cool and nonchalant about my son's sex life, but I think I might have butchered it."

"I'm certain I just heard Martin calling for you, Mother. It might be his rhododendrons again," Presti said.

"Oh, bollocks. I spoke to him just yesterday. They're never going to thrive if he leaves them to the full fury of the midday sun," Penelope muttered as she walked away.

"What's a Martin and his rhododendrons?" I asked.

"Our neighbour. He's been trying to grow rhododendrons for well over two years in an effort to woo his ex back. He refuses a sunshade for them though. Keeps harping to Mum about extending our back awning. Mum tells him that's exactly the reason Pristine ran off. He's too cheap."

"Oh."

"Mm. Of course, I do try to remind Mother that the poor man is on a fixed pension."

"You are quite wonderful, Presti." As soon as I uttered the words, I knew my compliment embarrassed Presti. That wonderful shade of crimson flushed his cheeks. Of course, he'd think he didn't deserve to be called remarkable.

"I'm sorry. I hope you're not too traumatised by my mother. She means well."

"She's almost as wonderful as her son," I replied. "I wasn't certain if I should come here. You didn't answer my last letter—"

"I most certainly did," Presti interjected. He had? I never received it. Lost in the post? Or purposely withheld? My vote would be on the latter, but that was something to worry about later.

"Perhaps it's waiting for me at home. Anyway, I am sorry if my arrival is causing trouble for you. That was never my intention, though I should have known better. Simple isn't really something I can do in my life."

Presti sighed. "When we returned from England, Jules Vern—real name—wanted to do a big article on me as a local celebrity. I agreed to an interview, but Jules… Well, he wanted dirt, a scandal. Days after the interview, I found him lurking behind the display of ball gags at F*ckingham Phallus. He was waiting to take an incriminating picture when I stopped for a chat with Silkie Bellbird." Presti stopped. He took a deep breath and my hand before continuing. "That was one day of unwanted media attention I had to endure. A harshly voiced 'Fuck off 'from both Silkie and me was sufficient to get Jules to back off. I suspect it wouldn't be quite so easy for you."

"I have no idea what most of that means."

"It means that my brief flirtation with paparazzi was horrific. I cannot imagine what your life must be like. So, I definitely will not judge you for your choices or actions."

"Thank you," I whispered.

"Now, Astrid and Larry will be back soon with dinner. Mum has made up your bed, and I'm just about to restock the bathroom with superior quality toilet paper, so we'll have nothing left to do but settle in for the Marie-never-said-that bake-a-thon night."

"Said what?" I asked, not caring that I didn't even know who Marie was.

Presti waved his hand about. "Doesn't matter. We'll bake enough sweet treats to take leftovers to Mrs Nichols's homeless shelter."

"Sounds…wonderful," I said and meant it. Charity work made up an enormous part of my life. Still, it usually involved me turning up and having my photo taken, cutting a ribbon, or giving a speech begging rich people to give away money they'd never even miss. I'd never really gotten my hands dirty doing the hard work.

"Do you cook, James?"

"Oddly enough, my mother taught both George and me. Nothing fancy, but we can feed ourselves."

"Mm." Presti nodded. "Ah, I feel I should tell you, or perhaps warn you, that Astrid does not follow recipes."

"She doesn't?"

Presti shook his head. "Not at all. She feels baking is an experience in creative expression. If this were the 1950s, when Astrid would be required to remain barefoot, pregnant, and in the kitchen, poor Larry would be doomed to a life of almost inedible meals. Or he'd need to be wealthy enough to hire a cook."

"It's a good thing we've evolved as a society. Larry might need to cook to keep them alive."

"Mm." Presti tilted his head, watching me thoughtfully. "We could do with some more evolving, but that's a discussion for another day. There is quite a lot to say about the devolving of humankind. For now, let's get you an apron."

"Apron?" I asked as I stood and followed Presti into the small kitchen. A large window overlooking a colourful garden took up an entire wall. The house, though small, sat on a large block. Trees and flowers covered most of the space, leaving only a small, grassed area. The garden looked thoughtfully planned and lovingly tended. A handful of outdoor chairs were scattered about to take advantage of the shade and the views.

The interior of their home was an eclectic mix of styles, colours, and fabrics. Photos covered blank walls, and cushions and throw rugs scattered about gave a warm, homey feel. The kitchen, painted a bright and sunny yellow, might be small, but it looked well-used and functional. Outdated cupboards and countertops gave the kitchen character, which it would have lacked with more modern fittings.

In short, the Jones family home looked and felt nothing like the cold, austere rooms of the palace. It *felt* as if a family, a close family, lived in it. As Goldilocks might say, it felt just right.

"Um," I murmured as I saw Penelope wearing an apron with two women's faces on it and the words, "Noice, different, unusual." Sequins of every colour bedazzled almost the entirety of the apron, which troubled me. What if they fell off, and we wound up eating a sparkly lasagne? Could you imagine the headlines? 'Prince James Chokes to Death on Coloured Sequins While Dining on Homemade Lasagne'. Laughable.

"Oh. It's just mum's *Kath & Kim* apron," Presti said after catching me gaping at the apron. "She collects them…aprons, not Kath and Kim."

"Are they relatives?" I asked, searching for familiar features in the women adorning the sequined apron.

"Mother and daughter," Presti answered.

"Your mother's mother?"

"What? No. Kath Day Night is Kim's mother. No relation to my mother."

"Kath Day Night?"

"Mm." Presti fussed about in a drawer and pulled out some more material. I could only assume they were more aprons.

He handed one to me. I nervously unfurled it, though it was sequin-free. Fortunately, my apron was nothing worse than slightly frilly with a rainbow unicorn hugging an oversized cupcake. Presti's apron, however…

"I'm sorry," I snorted, "but that person's head looks exactly like…um." I faltered. Could one say testicles in front of a man one was interested in dating? Not to mention that the man's mother was also present, and this was only their third meeting in person?

"Mm. A giant ball sac?" Presti said, looking entirely adorable as his ears flushed lava red. "It is quite unfortunate, but Mother insists it's someone famous." He ran his hands over the giant ball sac head on his apron as if thinking of a fond memory. Perhaps he and his mother had discussed the testicular appearance of the head on his apron many wonderful times.

"Why else would his face be on an apron?" Penelope asked.

"Because he looks like testicles," I suggested.

Both Penelope and Presti appeared briefly surprised before they burst into laughter. Joining with them felt like slipping under a soft, warm blanket on a cold winter night. Never in my life had I fallen into such camaraderie with a person—people—so easily or so quickly. I felt comfortable, able to be myself around the

Joneses. The connection I felt with these Kincumbrians was extraordinary.

My family loved me—I knew that. But our lives were rigid, so planned and full of duty to everyone and everything but us. We had no opportunity for spontaneous moments filled with debates and discussions on why a man who resembled testicles managed to get his image printed on an apron. Our conversations included discussions about plans and events and coordinating who represented the monarchy where and when, usually with our private secretaries involved.

I hadn't understood what I'd missed with my family until I experienced it with Presti. I'd been missing out on so much. My entire family had. My chest ached with a longing I hadn't fully understood until now.

"Oh, wonderful," Astrid cried as she and Larry burst into the kitchen carrying armfuls of shopping bags. "I'll take the operation, and Larry always looks incredibly sexy in the Barry Wood sitting in a flower field apron."

This was not the first time I had little idea what was being said, and before my visit here ended, I doubted it would be the last.

"I found this arsehole outside too," Astrid continued, motioning with her head somewhere over her left shoulder.

A black cat sauntered in, gazing about as if waiting for applause or possibly for us to bow to it. It very dexterously jumped onto the kitchen bench and glared at me with its large yellow eyes.

"Well, there you are, Johnny Sins," Presti crooned, reaching to scratch behind the cat's ears.

"Is your cat trying to hypnotise me?" I asked when the furry critter's eyes did not look away from me or blink after too long a period.

"He may be plotting your untimely demise," Presti answered, "but he hasn't mastered hypnotism as far as I know."

"Perhaps he has hypnotised you to forget that you know he can hypnotise you," offered Larry.

"This could be why you need to feed Johnny Sins a treat whenever you come home," Astrid added. "He has hypnotised you."

"I give him a treat because he is an adorable angel, not because he's taken control of my mind. And because cats think that's why their humans leave the home. In search of food. He thinks I'm out hunting for him, and disappointing him would be poor form."

"Why is your cat called Johnny Sins?" I asked.

"Named after Presti's favourite porn star," Larry answered.

"Oh," was the only response I managed.

"At least I did not call my cat *Cat*," Presti said.

"His name is Grimalkin," Larry said with the barest hint of frustration in his tone.

Presti sighed as though he'd had this conversation many times. "Which literally means a cat."

"I have a dog," I put in. "His name is Pad." Everyone continued to stare at me. "He has a fear of red socks. Runs as if the devil is on his tail if he catches me wearing them."

"We had a beagle once, Beagle Scout. He hated toilet paper. Couldn't leave a roll in the holder, or we'd find it torn up all over the unit," Astrid said.

"I'd like to get back to Grimalkin—"

"Shall we bake?" Astrid half asked, half shouted. "I do not wish to have this argument again."

"Why did you call your dog Pad?"

Again, that strange twinge of belonging pinched my insides, leaving me smiling as I began to answer Larry's question.

Some hours later, we fell exhausted into the outdoor setting in the courtyard behind the Jones home. We were covered in an assortment of baking ingredients, each with a plate of spaghetti Bolognese whipped up by Penelope and all with huge grins plastered to our faces.

We'd baked and talked and laughed. I'd felt like I'd always been part of this group, this family. Not for a moment had I been made to feel like an outsider or practical stranger.

"Your garden smells amazing," I said as I twirled more spaghetti around my fork. Johnny Sins cavorted about my legs, rubbing himself against my shins. Even he had taken to me, welcomed me as a friend.

"It's Presti's garden, really. He selected everything, planted it all and takes care of it," Penelope answered. "He's always coming home after one of his classes with new ideas."

"Flora is my speciality," Presti said.

"Well, you've certainly done a wonderful job. Your home is just… Well, it's a home if that makes sense."

"Perfectly," Penelope replied, smiling warmly at me.

"I'm an orphan," Larry yelled in something of a non sequitur. "Grew up in a string of foster homes." He stopped, grabbed Astrid's hand and kissed the back of it. "I had no idea what a home was, what family was. Then I met Astrid and her family, which includes more than her and her father. Penelope and Presti are her family too. Now, they're mine. Their home is my home."

"Isn't he wonderful?" Astrid asked us all. "Simply divine."

"Quite perfect," Presti agreed, leaving me a little—I am ashamed to admit—jealous.

"As?" Larry asked, voice gone low and gravelly. "Might we head home now?"

Astrid leapt to her feet. "I think we must."

And she and Larry left us in a swirl of blushed cheeks and knowing goodbyes. They weren't walked out as if they were mere guests. They saw themselves out because Larry was right, and this was their home too.

After their departure, we sat in silence, gazing at the stars, mulling through our thoughts, whatever they might be.

Then, Penelope said, "James, I know you're embroiled in something of a furore right now, but I hope you know that you are welcome here in this home, this family, for as long as you need."

"Thank you, Penelope. That means a lot to me."

She stood, patted my knee and said, "Well, you are very welcome. It's late and tonight has been… I'm not sure what to call it, but I'm going to head over to Howard's." Then she kissed Presti on his forehead, whispered goodnight, and left us alone.

"You have a wonderful family, Presti," I murmured after a time.

"I am fortunate. I know that. Poor Silkie lost her family because they refused to accept her as she was. Jason Southerland used to come to school every day covered in fresh bruises. Macy Fairclough's mother used to scream at her from the second she picked her up from school and likely kept it up until she dropped her back the next morning. Shelly and Ian Clovis always looked as if they and their clothes were never cleaned, and Byron Tomkins had the most haunted look in his eyes every single day. And they are just the ones where something was obviously terribly wrong in their home life."

"Jesus Christ."

"Mm. My point is I know how lucky I am, and I never take it for granted."

"May I ask about your father?"

Presti tensed but shrugged his shoulders incongruously as if his father's mention meant nothing to him. "I don't recall him at all. From what Mum told me, he was, or is, your garden variety loser. Nothing exceptional about him at all."

"There, I must disagree," I said. "He has a most exceptional son."

Though night had long since fallen, the blush creeping up Presti's throat to the tips of his ears was unmistakable. A small, shy smile ticked his lips in such a way he looked adorable. Thoroughly kissable.

"Tell me about your family?" Presti asked. "I mean, I've met your brother and father briefly. What are they like?"

"Well, like you, I can't complain. I know they love me, but they have such a weight on their shoulders, being the heirs. Honestly, I can't imagine what it's like."

"Are they… I mean, do they want to be king?"

"I don't think they've considered it, actually. They were told they'd be king one day from the day they were born. I'm not sure they've even thought about any other option." Neither had I, for that matter. I hadn't been raised to be king, but I hadn't had a say in any other option than being the spare and fulfilling a life of public duty.

"Heavy is the head that wears the crown," Presti mused. "I suppose the silver lining is they don't have the pressure of actually ruling."

"Thank god." I laughed. "I love my father and brother, but they'd make terrible rulers. Dad is sometimes a bit flighty, as Mum affectionately calls him. Tends to get lost in his books. If he didn't have a team to ensure he gets to where he's supposed to be, he'd never make it half the time."

"And George?"

"George is…sometimes cruel and thoughtless. He usually means well, but he lacks compassion at other times."

Along with the whole, 'your life will be one of public service and duty 'I'd grown up with, I'd also been deluged with warnings of keeping my mouth shut about my family. I'd been indoctrinated with a code of utter loyalty. To be speaking so openly with Presti about my family should terrify me and make me feel as if spiders were crawling under my skin. Instead, I felt relaxed and unburdened in a way I wasn't used to.

"And your mum?" Presti gamely asked.

"She lives for her charities, which is wonderful," I hastily added. "Sometimes, though, I miss her, I guess. What does that make me? What kind of person is jealous of the time their mother gives to charities?"

"A son who misses his mother," Presti murmured.

"But—"

"James." Presti reached for my hand and threaded his fingers between mine. "It doesn't make you a bad person to wish you could spend more time with your mother. It just means you're very much human."

The same urge, or maybe instinct, that had driven me to ask for Presti's kiss in my grandmother's clock room, rode me now. I brought our joined hands to my lips and kissed each of Presti's knuckles I could reach.

"Thank you," I whispered.

"You're welcome." Presti smiled softly. "You should get some sleep. You must be exhausted, and I have a big day planned for us tomorrow."

"Oh? Any hints?"

Presti stood, bent to kiss the tip of my nose and said, "Not a one."

My life had been suddenly upended, but with every passing second, I became more and more confident that I'd come to the perfect place and the perfect person to help me turn it right side up.

Chapter Thirteen

BRINGING JAMES HERE might not have been my best idea ever. But there were two things I knew for sure. First, the paparazzi were extremely unlikely to be hanging around outside the Home Strait Retirement Resort's weekly Scrabble tournament. And second, many of the scrabblers wouldn't be able to either see or hear well enough to recognise James or would forget they met him as soon as he left.

What I wasn't quite so certain about was if James would enjoy himself.

And from the look of consternation on his face as he, Astrid, Larry, and I marched through the doors of the Home Strait, I thought perhaps I'd talked up today just a smidge too much. Why on earth would a jet-setting prince accustomed to high society soirees ever be excited about spending a few hours playing a board game with a group of, admittedly wonderful, senior citizens.

Yet, everything inside me told me he needed this. Prince James needed to be *just* James, at least for a short while. He didn't need bowing, or polite words. He needed to be normal, to be treated as if he were normal. And we could give him that.

"Are we visiting your grandparents?" James asked.

James hadn't woken until almost nine this morning and I'd been content to let him sleep. Flying halfway around the world tended to be exhausting, from my limited experience, not to mention the emotional strain of James's unfortunate outing. But when he'd finally arisen, showered, and dressed, James looked luminous. I'd never seen a more devastatingly beautiful person in all my days and doubted I ever would again.

And now, as I watched his curious gaze dart around the room, I couldn't help but feel a little breathless. Despite my best intentions, nothing about this was normal. "No," I answered, offering James a smile. "We're playing our weekly Scrabble tournament against Seamus O'Hare's Words of a Feather and Maureen Dixon's Dixonaries."

"Oh, um. May I ask the name of your team?"

"Mother's Little Scrabblers."

James nibbled adorably at his bottom lip. "And will I be playing in one of these teams?"

"Oh yes," replied Astrid. "We've been playing a player down since a vote held that my father couldn't play remotely due to Mary Whittle's firm conviction that technology is the devil's tool."

"Does your father live far?"

"Not at all, "Astrid replied. "He lives with me. Unfortunately, he suffers from agoraphobia."

"Oh. I'm sorry."

"No need to be, but thank you."

"Your mother doesn't play, Presti?"

"Ah, she is currently on a three-week ban." My ears warmed as a flush crept up my throat. "She used a few too many…indelicate words."

"To be fair," Astrid defended, "I hardly think hussy is worth banishment for three weeks."

"It wasn't hussy that pushed them over the edge though." I hoped James wouldn't ask what word my mother had spelled out with her tiles. I did not relish cussing before royalty.

"So, no indelicate words then." James smiled. "Got it."

"And don't stare," Larry added.

"Stare?"

"Mm. At Seamus. He was young and foolish. Thought he was in love. I guess it is kind of romantic and how was he to know they'd never grow back," I explained.

"What wouldn't?" James asked, his expression adorably curious.

"His eyebrows. His first girlfriend suffered from trichophobia. Absolutely paralysed with fear at the sight of hair up close. Must have been extraordinarily difficult, given most people tend to be rather well covered and then there's the positively hirsute." I'd thought about poor Seamus's girlfriend quite a lot, more than I should, but how did she manage day to day in a world of follicularly thriving humans? "So, Seamus…de-haired himself. Sadly, his eyebrows never grew back."

"Poor Seamus."

"Mm. He tends to draw his brows on but even after all this

time he's not terribly good at it. Looks constantly surprised actually."

"Well." James smiled softly. "I'll be certain not to stare."

"I guess you are used to it. Not staring, I mean. You must meet all sorts of people." I couldn't imagine having to do the things James does as a prince of England. Meeting one or two strangers I found challenging enough, but having to meet the sheer volume James did blew my mind.

"I do meet all kinds, and as hard as I find it, it has also shown me how wonderfully diverse our world is."

"Brace yourself, Presti," Astrid groaned. "Here comes Peter Gussett."

"Oh, lord help us," I muttered and then said to James, "Poor Peter always mistakes me for an old army buddy. Forever trying to grab me and hurl me into a foxhole."

"Booney? What the devil are you doing? Get yourself back in that foxhole before you get your head blown off." Peter ordered as he grabbed my arm and attempted to launch me across the room into the safety of a foxhole invisible to the rest of us.

"Right you are," I replied, attempting something like a graceful dive to the floor.

"Bloody stupid young bugger," Peter groused but continued on his way, apparently satisfied I was safe from harm now that I'd landed spreadeagled on the floor.

James offered me a chivalrous hand up once Peter had gone. His strong grip emphasised the warmth and softness of his hands. I did not often get lecherous thoughts while visiting the Home Strait, but how could I not when a devastatingly handsome prince held my hand?

"Thank you," I whispered. Self-preservation warned me not to get too attached, too besotted with Prince James. All too soon he'd return to England, to his life, and where would that leave me if he took my heart with him?

"Shall we?" Astrid asked after I'd stood frozen and staring at the prince for far too long.

"Of course."

The games room had been set up exactly as it was every other Saturday afternoon with a handful of tables topped with Scrabble boards. A trolley sat along the far wall with plates of biscuits and a hot water urn for the numerous cups of tea we consumed during our matches. Our fellow competitors were already seated and ready to play. I quickly introduced James, hoping if I went fast enough nobody would have time to look too closely at our new player.

Once we were seated and the games underway, I released a relieved breath. Our subterfuge appeared to be working. No one had given James more than a cursory look. No one gasped with recognition of royalty in their midst.

And James seemed to be having the time of his life.

"Should we intervene?" James leaned over his board where he fought a healthy battle against Seamus. He stared, quite alarmed, at Astrid who engaged in a heated debate with Mary Whittle, self-proclaimed judge and jury of the Scrabble tournament.

"Best to leave them to it, actually. I suspect Mary is questioning one of Astrid's word choices. She refuses to accept any word not found in her *Macquarie Dictionary*, and as you are aware, Astrid has a most unique knowledge of rare words." I leaned a little close and continued, "You should hear Mary when Oliver uses made-up words from pop culture."

"Such as?"

"Well, things almost came to blows when he tried using Arrakis."

"Like from *Dune*?"

"Exactly." One of the things I liked about James was his ability to follow my conversations wherever they might lead. I didn't know who to thank for his gift because I frequently managed to confuse others. "Are you having a good time?"

James flicked his gaze to where Seamus was placing his tiles, gave him a little glare, then turned back to me. "I'm having the best time. Though where do we stand on what I can only guess are Dutch words?"

"Absolutely not allowed and Seamus knows that," I said. Seamus gave me a smirk and a wink before returning his attention to his tiles.

"How did this start?" James waved his hands about to encompass the room and everyone and thing in it.

"Oh, well, Astrid and I chose community service rather than playing sports in high school. Neither of us are particularly athletic. Mr Rubenhold sent us here and we enjoyed ourselves very much."

James gave me one of those smiles where it looked as if he couldn't quite figure me out but seemed to like me regardless. "Not many people your age would spend their Saturday afternoons at a Scrabble tournament."

"Mm. I suspect they'd rather be out drinking or partying."

"Oh, cripes," Muriel Spranger, my opponent, muttered.

"Don't give this one drinks. Next thing you know he'll be standing on the railway overpass brandishing an imaginary sword as he prepares to fight off the invading French."

"That happened one time!" I protested. I could not believe this episode was being brought up again and this time in front of James.

Unrepentant, Muriel continued," Thought he was Henry the bloody Fifth at Agincourt."

"Actually, I thought I was one of his knights," I replied, ridiculously aggrieved that she was telling my tale incorrectly. I should be insisting on her silence.

"By the time I got there," Larry interjected, "Presti was screaming that it was his duty to die for the king and my lovely Astrid was shouting right back that no, it was his duty to live for her."

James barked a laugh. "Was she drunk too?"

"Nope," Larry answered. "That's just how they are. Love one and you must love the other."

"Not in the sense of a thruple-type situation," I added. "We don't, well, I just, I mean sex with one person is…well, it's enough, isn't it? But throw in another set of hands, and, well, you know, an extra penis or vagina. Where would everything go?"

The games room of the Home Strait Retirement Resort went very still and deathly silent.

Until finally Astrid said, "I don't think Larry was alluding to us being a thruple, Presti. And it's entirely possible you've just given Mary a small heart attack."

"Apologies, Mary. Small misunderstanding." Even as I made my apology, many of the other residents, excluding Mary, roared with laughter. James did that lovely lopsided smile of his and played around with his tiles, a faint bloom of pink colouring his cheeks. Despite my humiliation, I couldn't see past how lovely James looked.

"You mustn't worry, Presti. We all have our stories," Seamus said, still trying to leash his laughter. "I bet James here has some of his own. Stuff like that makes us human, endearing. Right, James?"

"Yes. It's a wonderful story. I'm only sorry I wasn't there to witness it."

"Two vodkas and he'll likely re-enact it for you," Astrid added, earning herself a 'do shut up 'glare from me.

"That is a gross fabulousity, Astrid. I'd had at least four vodkas, and it was the first time I'd ever touched alcohol."

"Might we get back to the tournament," Mary Whittle admonished. "We don't have all day; we are on the home straight after all."

"Right you are," Seamus agreed, and we all focused our attention back to our Scrabble boards.

Except I noticed James staring at me every now and then with a look I couldn't quite decipher on his face. Whenever I caught him, he'd smile that crooked grin, his eyes would soften, and he'd turn back to his Scrabble tiles.

James's fixed attention on me produced a bout of aprosexia as my distracted mind couldn't focus at all on Scrabble. Instead, I tried to decide what James's staring meant and if I should be happy about it.

Of Mother's Little Scrabblers, only Astrid won her game, but none of us cared. We'd talked and laughed with each other, bickered over silly words and accusations of cheating. It had been a wonderful day, but then, they always were at the Home Strait Scrabble tournaments.

Astrid, Larry, James, and I walked silently home, Astrid and Larry hand in hand and a few steps ahead. Dark clouds of an incoming storm blotted out the stars and moon, leaving an ink-black sky. Street lights glowed eerily through the mist. Though winter was behind us, it wasn't hot yet.

Despite the wonderful day, a tremor of sadness rippled through me. We'd been attending these Scrabble tournaments for six years. We'd seen faces come and go. Loss was no stranger to me. Yet the idea that I might not see James's smiling face at next Saturday's game tore a little rip in my heart. And it surprised me how much it hurt.

"Are you all right, Presti?"

Embarrassingly, I jumped as James's voice broke the silence. I glared at him. "Cyril Horton died fifteen minutes after he lost a particularly intense game of Scrabble against me. Felice Stevens died an hour before the tournament one week. People die, James."

"Um, yes. I am quite aware."

"Or they leave because they don't like being around you anymore. Or they get a new job interstate. Or perhaps they fall in love and move to be closer to their lover. Maybe they want to live somewhere warmer or colder."

"Presti?"

"My point is, James, people leave. And you'll leave." My voice cracked a little on the end there, but I didn't care. Why shouldn't James know I'd miss him when he left. "And, well, I already know that I shall miss you when you do."

James stopped, and as if we were joined together by a piece of twine, I did too. "I will have to go home one day. And I shall miss you too."

"We can resume our penpalship," I suggested.

"I would like that very much." James smiled, reached out, and tentatively cupped my cheek, his thumb brushing against my skin.

Yes. Dear god, yes. I would miss him awfully.

Once we'd said goodnight to Astrid and Larry, James and I walked home mostly in silence. We didn't need to fill the quiet with words to feel comfortable. That was a rare thing, especially for two people who hadn't known each other very well. James and I fit... We worked. Feeling so relaxed with another person felt like a precious gift, and I intended to jealously guard this new relationship.

As we walked, our arms brushed. James's fingers sought out mine, held them gently. We were holding hands. We were friends, pen pals. I didn't really know what label to give us, but whatever we were, I was happy. James held my hand, and I was happy.

Simple.

"You really wrote back to me?" James whispered in the dark.

"I did."

James sighed heavily. "Simon probably intercepted it."

"Pardon?" Had I stepped into a Romeo and Juliette situation where evil forces would strive to keep us apart? Ridiculous.

"Simon de Montfort is Gran's personal secretary. He's a weasel. Cares only about the monarchy, and I very much doubt he's pleased with our...writing to each other."

"He's trying to stop our penpalship?"

"Penpalship?" James asked. He began swinging our arms as if we were the happiest two people on earth. Maybe we were.

"Mm. Astrid and I dubbed it as such. Well, the evil Simon may be trying to thwart us, but I have the drafts of that letter in my scrapbook" — *oh, god* — "if you wish to read it."

"You're keeping a scrapbook?" James's tone stayed light, but I hoped I hadn't scared him with that revelation.

"James," I began. "I know this is no surprise to you, but you are a prince."

"Yes. Yes, I am aware."

"Well it is something of a novelty for me. I've never met royalty before — if we don't include my birth at the feet of your grandmother. So, I'm keeping souvenirs of this wondrous turn of events. Silly, I know, but one day I might look back and think this was all some kind of very vivid dream. At least I'll have the scrapbook to remind me it was real. *You* were real."

James stopped walking. I matched him as if we were one. I turned to face him, watched the moonlight flash in his soft eyes, saw the hint of a smile on his lovely mouth. He stole my breath with his beauty.

"I'm real, Presti. This is real." And then he leant in, pressing his soft lips to mine in the gentlest of kisses.

I pressed back, harder, searching for more. Needing more. James's arms circled my waist, hauled me closer. Our bodies touched everywhere. The feel of him so close, every ridge and hard plane against mine was incredible. I wished there were a way we could stay like this forever.

My fingers twisted in his hair, lightly tugging, pushing, pulling as I held on, hoping the kiss would never end.

Of course, it did end. When it did, we were both breathless. James's eyes shone with desire. Nobody had ever looked at me like that before. It was exhilarating. Life-changing.

I'd found people attractive before, but I'd never felt such desire, such unrestrained want for someone. As amazing as I felt, I knew the danger. This was not a simple boy-likes-boy situation.

With James's kiss still fresh on my lips, I knew we were heading into territory we might not come back from unscathed.

But I simply did not care.

James was worth the risk.

Chapter Fourteen

ONE WEEK I'D been hiding out at Presti's. As much as I enjoyed my seclusion, my will wasn't strong enough to stop me looking at what the press had to say about my disappearance. They had daily updates. Speculation ran the gamut from a simple case of me lying low to let things settle down after the infamous photo, to theories I'd been hustled off to some kind of pray-the-gay-away camp.

My family maintained their dignified silence. Though they'd reached out to me, I'd only sent text replies. I wasn't ready to hear their voices. I couldn't stand the thought of hearing underlying disappointment in me.

Presti had offered to skip classes and spend the days with me. As much as I'd wanted his company, I'd declined his offer though. I refused to be more of a burden to him than I already was. If the press found out I was here, his life would blow up in ways he could not begin to imagine. Truthfully, only a small miracle had allowed me to remain undiscovered for this long.

While I missed Presti's calming presence during the days, at least I could comfort myself that the nights were ours. Penelope remained at Howard's and Astrid, too, appeared to be keeping her distance. Perhaps they'd made an agreement to give us some privacy. While I relished the time alone with him, I did not want Presti's family to feel as if they had to stay away.

In fact, we'd had something like an argument about it. Each stood our ground until we'd agreed to spend time with Astrid and Larry at her father's house tonight. I wasn't afraid to admit I was looking forward to it. I refused to upend Presti's life more than I had.

Over the last six days, I'd, perhaps foolishly, let Presti chip away at the walls entrenched around my heart. I'd cracked the door, and he'd barged right in. In my guts I knew this could only lead to hurt, but I was helpless to stop him.

I was still searching for the courage to confirm the rumours about me, let alone present a boyfriend to the world. And how would Presti cope with the invasion of his privacy? Would he even want to? What were the chances he'd find me worthy enough to upend his life for?

Yes, we'd spent a wonderful week together. We'd talked, some nights until the early morning hours. We'd even made out several times on the couch before bed, soft lazy kisses, unhurried, easy. Every moment we spent together had been comfortable.

But if we went public, if I asked Presti to be with me, his life would never be the same. The microscope of public opinion and intrusion would consume everything and everyone Presti cared about. How could I possibly be worth that? How could I ask him to even consider that?

"James," Presti murmured, slipping up behind me and wrapping his arms around my waist. His breath tickled my nape, his lips barely touching my skin there. "What are you pondering?"

Every cell in my body flared to living colour at his touch, my soul stretching toward his. I wanted to be honest with him, to share my hopes and fears. But how could I be the cause of his ruin? And I knew being in the public eye might well destroy this wonderful, amazing man. I felt on the verge of destruction from it myself, and I'd been born into it, raised to live with the odd curiosity people had with royalty.

"I think…well, it may be time for me to go home," I answered, the words like ash on my tongue.

"So soon," Presti murmured.

"I've hidden for over a week. I should go."

"You don't need to leave on our account, James. We're all very happy to have you with us." Presti released me, then circled around to face me. A soft blush shaded his handsome face, illuminating the spattering of freckles across his nose. My god, he took my breath away every single time I laid eyes on him.

"I, especially, like having you here," he added.

"I like being here, too, but I have a life to get back to, Presti. A duty."

He stiffened, a bloom of hurt bursting in the blue of his eyes. "Yes, of course." Presti cleared his throat, straightened his already ramrod straight spine. "When shall you go?"

As much as I knew my words hurt him, I also knew this was

a small ache compared to the agony trying to share a life with me would bring to him. I would bear the pain of his loss because I would not survive hurting Presti more. "In the next day or two. I haven't made arrangements yet, but it's time."

Presti nodded, clenching his fists as if pulling himself together. "Well, for now, then, let's visit Astrid and Paul as promised." He turned and marched toward the front door. After the Scrabble tournament he'd very clearly expressed his concern about my eventual departure. We'd both known it would happen; we weren't stupid. But I should not have allowed us to get so close in the meantime.

"As promised," I muttered.

The walk to Astrid's small unit over a sex shop was painfully quiet. I didn't know how to fix things with Presti, and maybe it would be better, easier for him, if I didn't try. If he hated me, he wouldn't hurt when I left.

"I didn't mean to hurt you, Presti," I said as we took the stairs up to Astrid's door. He had to know I'd rather set myself on fire than hurt him.

He jumped as if I'd startled him from his thoughts. "Nonsense. I am not hurt. I wasn't expecting your departure, which makes me something of a ninnyhammer because, of course, you must go home. Your family must be quite frantic with worry. I was being selfish wanting you to stay, because I will miss you."

"Please don't say that," I whispered, my will to leave his side weakening, though I knew I must.

"Why not? It's true. Not many people stay in my life, James. Not many want to, so I tend to jealously hoard the ones who do."

"Anybody…" I said, stepping forward to close the distance

between us. "Anybody who does not wish to have you in their life is the ninnyhammer, Presti." My fingers curled around the back of his neck as I eased him closer. His lips were warm and yielding against mine as he accepted my kiss. Christ, I would miss this.

But I could not see a way to keep Presti and leave his happiness intact.

"Well, I wasn't expecting to happen upon this little spectacle," Larry said, interrupting us as he came up the stairs. "Astrid will be most vexed she missed it."

"We are not a public spectacle," Presti said with a smile in his voice.

"Then you shouldn't bloody well pash in a public locale." Larry winked.

"Yes. Right. Quite true." Presti fumbled and fidgeted, yet at least didn't seem to regret our kiss.

Larry laughed and edged past us to open the door to Astrid's home.

"You have a key?" Presti blurted.

"Oh yes. There was a ceremony and everything. She gave it to me in a velvet-lined box. Said it was more important than a wedding ring, given that marriage is a dead institution," Larry answered as we stepped inside.

"It is?" I asked. Nobody had informed me of the demise of matrimony.

"Mm," Presti replied, as he often did. To Larry he said, "You know she still wants to marry you."

"And she shall," Larry answered just as Astrid rounded the corner and stepped into his waiting arms. "Caught these two pashing at the front door."

"Ooh, how delightful. I must say this thing between you two has exceeded all my expectations." Astrid gave a little clap.

"It has?" Presti questioned just as I asked, "What expectations?"

"Well, it must be like a fairy tale, mustn't it? There is a prince and a commoner facing all sorts of obstacles to be together and find their happy ever after."

"Oh god," Presti groaned.

I…well, I couldn't think of a thing to say. Because this wasn't a fairy tale and there would be no happy ever after for Presti and me. Not together anyway. I still hoped Presti would find someone one day who could make him happy, keep him happy. That person wasn't me. Prince James could not make Presti happy.

"Astrid, you're mortifying His Highness. Tone it down a notch." An older man with eyes that were identical to his daughter's came into the room.

Paul Bomalier, silver-haired, tall and striking, was the silveriest fox I'd ever met. I mean, this man should be on the cover of *GQ*. He'd give George Clooney a run for his money. And I couldn't stop staring at him.

"I believe the word you're looking for is '*wow* '," Presti said, smirking and raising his eyebrows.

"Yes. I mean…" I trailed off, unwilling to add anything further to this already awkward conversation.

"Right? I've said it many times, but you are a fox, Mr Bomalier." Presti laughed and hugged Astrid's father.

"And if I was twenty years younger…and gay?" Paul responded.

Astrid rolled her eyes fondly. "You two are ridiculous."

"It's good to meet you, Your Highness," Paul said, offering his hand to me.

I shook it and replied, "Please, just call me James. It's good to meet you too."

"Come on in."

We followed behind Paul, Astrid and Larry arm in arm, Presti silent at my side.

Though smaller than Presti's home, the unit had as much warmth and homeyness. Books were everywhere: in cases, stacked on the floor, covering tables. There must have been thousands of them.

"You have an amazing collection of books," I said.

"They're mine and Astrid's really. We are both bibliophiles. Do you read much, James?" Paul asked as he gestured to a seat for me.

"Not as much as I'd like. My time isn't really my own."

Paul took the seat opposite me, Presti at my side, Astrid almost in Larry's lap in the armchair. "No, I suppose it's not," Paul replied. "Must be difficult."

"There are definitely some things I want but can't have because of who I am." My gaze flicked to Presti despite my order for it not to. "I shouldn't complain though. There are worse lives I could lead."

"But there could be better," Paul said wistfully. "I know quite well about having your choices taken away from you. If it weren't for my agoraphobia, I'd be living a different life, even though, like you, I know mine could be worse."

I offered Paul a smile. He was an incredibly attractive man

and seemed lovely. I could only imagine what his life might be if not for his agoraphobia.

"Enough of that though," Paul said. "Dinner is almost ready, and then we'll play charade karaoke."

"I don't know that game."

"It's easy. We'll explain." Presti turned to Paul. "Dare I hope you've cooked your amazing carbonara?"

"Of course." Paul smiled. "Would I serve you anything else?"

"No. But I do worry Astrid may hijack the kitchen."

Talk descended into a mock argument about Astrid's skill in the kitchen and somehow morphed into something of a competition over who amongst them was best at a variety of skills. Easy, kind-hearted conversation and fun. These types of interactions I rarely had with anyone but most especially not my family.

Growing up in the palace, I knew, of course, my family was different in many ways from most others, but I'd never felt that difference more acutely than over this past week. I wanted what Presti and his family had. Desperately.

However, what I wanted and what I got were often two different things.

"So, we're really going to sing?" I asked, desperate for a distraction from yearning for all things Presti. Where he was concerned, I'd leapt head first into dangerous territory. The time for being careful with my feelings had passed before I'd even realised there was danger in being around Presti.

"Oh yes," Presti answered. "Don't worry if you don't sing well. It could not be worse than Paul's!"

"Hey! My singing isn't that bad," Paul groused.

"It isn't that good either," Astrid replied.

"I think he has quite a lovely, melodic voice," Larry added.

Paul barked a laugh. "There is no need to truckle, Larry. I already approve of you dating my daughter." Paul leaned over to ruffle Larry's hair, his eyes glowing as he looked at his daughter.

"Yes. You approve…now, but we all recall the fiasco of introductory dinner 2022." Astrid smiled.

"Hey. It was not my fault. I was choking on spinach."

"Poor Larry regurgitated much of his meal on Paul's lap," Presti whispered to me.

"Oh."

"Mm. Quite a…sticky situation."

Listening to Presti, to Larry, Astrid, and Paul, and listening to every interaction during the last week, I couldn't decide if it was wrong of me to be jealous or not. All I knew for certain was that my heart had this tear, a little ache which seemed to be growing. I yearned for something, maybe Presti—I knew I wanted him—maybe the close connection he shared with his family and friends. All I knew was I yearned for something urgently. I needed to satiate this need, or it might just kill me.

A little dramatic perhaps, but I wanted to mend the rip in my heart. I wanted to be filled with warmth and friendship and love. And I had a healthy suspicion that Presti was the key. But in reaching for my happiness, would I destroy Presti's? That was the question I didn't know—didn't want to know—the answer to.

Dinner was amazing. Not just the food, the company also. Though it was still early, this felt like the best night of my life. I never wanted it to end, yet I knew it was coming. Home and duty called to me, a soft whisper that was getting louder every day.

"Are you ready for charade karaoke?" Presti asked as we cleared the table.

"Explain it to me?"

"Quite simple. Choose a song and a book. Sing the song but exchange the words for the first page or so of the book. Winner is first to pick either the song or book title. Double points if you pick both." Presti leaned over to pack the dishwasher, but he looked back up at me, and his smile was…blinding.

"I don't know the words of any book like that." My god, I predicted making a colossal fool of myself in my near future.

"Oh no, well, of course not. Who does? Except Paul, but we can use an iPad. Paul has thousands of books on it."

I watched Presti as he worked. Light and shadows flickering on the supple muscles of his arms, his thighs. He was beautiful. So damn beautiful. Inside and out. I craved his beauty, wanted to hoard it for myself, stay in the orbit of his loveliness for as long as I could.

"Okay. I'll play…if, if you swear to me, you will not laugh at me."

Presti froze, his body rigid with tension. "Is that what you think of me?" He would not turn around, would not look at me.

"No. No, I didn't mean… I'm sorry, Presti. I shouldn't have said that."

"I've been laughed at my entire life, James. I always knew they were laughing at me, even when people tried to hide it. I don't care, not anymore, but I'd never laugh at others. Not when I know how much it can hurt."

Jesus.

"Presti, look at me. Please."

Slowly, he turned around, his eyes shining, the moonlight catching the glow. So damn beautiful. I took a gentle step toward him. Slow. Hesitant. My finger stroked the soft skin of his cheek; my palm cupped the warm flesh.

"I'm so sorry," I whispered, then leaned in closer. "You take my breath away, Presti. I've never met anybody like you." A soft sigh escaped from Presti's lips, a gentle want. I kissed him then. With all the need I felt for him.

Our bodies pressed together, his fingers in my hair, mine in his. Christ, I wanted him. "Presti," I gasped.

"Mm." His murmur vibrated through me; his scent surrounded me. His presence in my arms consumed me, and I never wanted to part from him again.

But how could I drag him into my world? How could I let the press and the public rip him apart, sour his sweetness? They would pick him to pieces and devour whatever remained.

There'd be tomorrow to think about leaving him, to worry how I'd ever survive the separation. Tonight, I wanted to enjoy myself, enjoy him. I pressed my lips to his again, kissed him with everything I had in me. Revelled in the feeling of him melting under my touch. His heated skin against mine felt like a match to tinder. A few more minutes of this and I'd combust.

"I am sorry to interrupt," Astrid said after clearing her throat, "but we must begin. Poor Larry has work early in the morning, and if he doesn't get his eight hours..."

Presti groaned, matching my own frustrated sigh. "Very well. Shall we draw straws?"

"We already have. You're up first, Presti."

"Wonderful. Let's begin. Come on, James."

I followed Presti back into the warmly furnished living room and took my seat. For a moment, Presti stood before us, silent and contemplative, his eyes closed. Then he opened them, looked directly at me and began to sing.

His voice was beautiful, mesmerizing, but, then, to me, everything about him was. He'd never make a career singing, but he could hold a tune. I closed my eyes and listened. The strength of his voice filled me, wrapping me up in a world made up of nothing but Presti. He cocooned me, sheltered me from the crazy that had been all I'd known before I met this strange boy with the unusual name and the brilliant way of living his life.

Oh god.

I was falling for him.

"'Resolution 'is the song!" Astrid shouted.

"*The Great Gatsby* is the book," Larry yelled barely a second later.

Presti smiled his blinding smile and laughed his intoxicating laugh. And I fell thoroughly under his spell.

Paul went next and then Larry. Though they both sang tolerably well, they were nothing to Presti. Jesus, I couldn't take my mind off him. Astrid stood to take her turn, and I pried my gaze from Presti. Just as she began to sing, a phone rang. Paul jumped up to answer it.

Whoever called, they brought a smile to Paul's lips. At first. Then he frowned, his gaze darting to mine, holding there. Something was wrong.

"He is," Paul said. "Silkie…okay."

"Dad? "Astrid asked when Paul ended the call and came to stand before us.

"That was Silkie," he muttered, his gaze now unable to land on me.

"And?" Astrid pressed.

"She says the media is here. Downstairs. Outside her store. They've been asking her where Prince James is."

Oh god.

"They know he's here?" Presti asked, his tone panicked.

"Apparently."

"What do we do?" Larry asked. Nobody would look my way.

"I'm not sure." Finally, Paul glanced at me. "He's welcome to stay here, of course. But I don't think he wants to hide out in Kincumber forever."

Yes. I do.

"We could call in a bomb threat," Astrid said. "Draw their attention elsewhere."

"I'm quite sure they're not those kinds of journalists, my dear," Larry answered. "I'd wager nothing, regardless how big of a drama it was, could divert their attention."

"We could call the police to have them removed," offered Presti. "Constable Dickens has quite forgiven me for that unfortunate incident. He'd come to our aid."

"I'm so sorry," I whispered. How could such a wonderful time turn into a nightmare in the space of a second.

Presti stood, walked to me, and kneeled at my feet, his warm hands gripped mine where they rested in my lap. He'd be able to feel me trembling, but there was nothing I could do to stop it. "This is not your fault, James." He lifted my hands, kissed my knuckles. "You have nothing to be sorry for."

"I brought my crazy to your doorstep. They won't leave any of you alone now."

"Unless we can convince them you were never here," Paul said.

"How? They must have been tipped off. Perhaps they already have a photo of me coming and going. They might have been stalking me this whole time."

"Silkie seemed to think they didn't know much at all. She's coming up to see what she can do."

"Oh god," Presti groaned. "She's going to kill me for not telling her about you."

"You'd best brace yourself, James," Larry added. "Silkie can be…a lot."

As if conjured by our discussion of her, there was a knock at the door. Paul stalked out of the room to answer it but was back in seconds with an aging drag queen in tow.

"Oh my," she gasped breathily, fanning herself dramatically. "It's true then."

Silke strode further into the room, her large eyes locked on mine. She curtsied so low I wondered if she'd get back up again. When she did, she pointed to where Presti kneeled on the floor but did not look at him. "You, I will deal with later," she snapped. "But for now, let's get the prince out of here."

"How?" Presti asked.

"Has anybody ever seen *The Birdcage*?

Chapter Fifteen

JAMES MADE AN ugly woman.

And despite the dire situation we found ourselves in, I couldn't stop laughing every time I looked his way.

"Prestidigitation Jones," Silkie fumed. "If you laugh one more time, I shall become positively homicidal."

"Don't murder him on my account, Ms Bellbird," James crooned, his charm thick in the air. Who on this planet had the power to say no to him?

Silkie, astonishingly, blushed. "Well, my prince, for you I will leave him intact." Silkie bowed low for maybe the fiftieth time since she'd arrived.

"I am sorry, Silkie. But you must admit James, in fact all of us, look quite ridiculous." I frowned down at my outfit. A full-length gold-sequinned gown did nothing for my figure, though it hugged my body like a glove. I looked like an oddly shaped disco ball.

As hideous as my outfit was, it was nothing to the feathered monstrosity James had squeezed into. It had a flaming red, plunging neckline which Silkie planned to cover with a feather boa, because no self-respecting queen would allow a hairy cleavage to be on display. And then there were the wigs and make-up. Don't get me wrong, I'd seen Silkie in these frocks before, and she looked amazing in them. They just weren't for everyone.

Astrid cast a considering gaze over me. "You look good as a blonde, Presti. Perhaps you should—"

"You wash your mouth out. I was born a brunette and a brunette I shall remain."

"But blondes have more fun, apparently." Larry put his arm around Astrid and pulled her into his side. He too had been tizzied up into a skintight evening gown, his face painted with inch-thick make-up like the rest of us. Somehow, though, Larry managed to look pretty.

"You mustn't dye your hair, Presti," James murmured. Since news of his discovery broke, he'd been quiet and sullen, apologising repeatedly for the mess he'd got us all into. "The rich brown, almost black, of your hair is… Well, it's a lovely colour." James winced and shook his head sadly.

Was he so very distressed about our predicament or had he been unable to express himself adequately? I'd wager a bit of both.

"Silkie, how in the devil do you function with these eyelashes? It is like peering through slats in vertical blinds," I said to draw attention from James. Everything I knew about James warned me to keep the conversation light, nothing deep or troubling would do for this situation. As amazing and strong as I knew James to be, he also had a fragility that seemed to awaken a protective streak hibernating within me. I hadn't known it existed until I'd felt an overwhelming urge to knock out the teeth of the paparazzi waiting outside ready to pounce on James.

"Oh, my dear sweet boy," Silkie cooed, apparently troubled by my naivety where eyelashes were concerned. "These eyelashes are not there for functional purposes. They are a weapon in one's arsenal for seduction. Flutter, flutter, and pop." She did something weird with her eyes that, I'm not going to fib, frightened me a little.

"Or," Silkie continued. "One can look demurely up through one's lashes at the focus of one's desire." More than the flutter, flutter, and pop, I found Silkie's attempt at demure even more terrifying, but I knew she was trying to help. God, I loved her.

"Um, are we expected to…and pop?" James asked.

For a moment, I hoped the answer was yes. I really wanted to see James flutter and pop. But more than that, I wanted to see him smiling and happy like he'd been before Silkie called Paul to let him know James's world had blown up again.

"It couldn't hurt," Silkie answered. "Let's practice. Now, bat your lashes as if trying to dislodge grit from your eyeballs and then suddenly freeze with them wide open, looking up and to the side. This is your basic coy flutter, flutter, and pop."

Astoundingly, James did exactly as Silkie instructed. I'd never seen anything more adorable. "Like this?" James asked, fluttering and popping again and again.

Silkie clapped her hands and laughed. "Exactly like that. You are utter perfection, Your Highness."

James smiled back and then fluttered and popped in my direction. He mesmerized me, and it wasn't the first time since he'd landed on my doorstep. James had told me he'd never met anyone like me before; the same was obviously true for me. How would I survive him walking out of my life? But what reason did he have to stay?

"So, what's the plan?" Paul asked, still in his chinos and tee. As much as he wanted to, there'd be no fleeing the scene with us for Paul. I couldn't imagine a more wretched life than being trapped indoors. He had the occasional small victories, managing to walk downstairs and spend a few moments on the street, but they were few and far between.

"Well," Silkie began, throwing herself into the role of escape planner. "I've already laid the foundations for our cover story. I let slip to one of the vultures that I was in the middle of a drag class when they accosted me—"

"A drag class?"

"Sometimes, Astrid dear, fabulousness must be taught. One is not born with the ability to gracefully sashay in five-inch heels."

"That tall?" James stammered. He held up the heels Silkie had given him, glaring at them as if they offended him with their height.

"It is a must. No queen would be caught dead in less than five inches." Silkie winked, thankfully forgoing any further gymnastics with her eyelids.

"I'm not certain I can walk in these," James muttered.

"Forget walking in them. By the time I'm finished with you, Your Highness, you'll be effortlessly gliding in them."

An hour later, we were preparing to face the media in our

disguises. The chances of success had been thoroughly debated, the pros and cons of attempting this subterfuge endlessly picked apart. At the end of the day, it was all up to James whether we went through with it or not. He had the most to lose.

If we were discovered, I'd be in the media spotlight for a flicker of time, but for James, the scrutiny would never end. He'd be chased, hounded, his life picked apart. Every action, word he spoke, look he gave for the rest of his life would be debated, frowned upon. *Who* he was would be celebrated by some, vilified by others.

The life he led, the choices he had to make, the sacrifices, were far from enviable. Poor James. I simply could not imagine walking in his shoes, not even for a second.

"Presti?"

"Mm?"

James stepped closer, his breath ghosting over my skin, a shiver ripping up my spine at his nearness. "You can stay here. Nobody ever has to see you with me."

"Absolutely not. We leave no man behind, James." I furrowed my brow, willing my expression to show the determination I felt to stand by him even though my legs felt hollowed out and stuffed with jelly.

"We aren't going into battle," James replied, that beautiful smirk on his handsome face.

"Aren't we? I'd fight the whole damn world if it kept that frown from your lips," I declared, not caring I sounded like a fool.

"What frown? I'm smiling."

"Now, yes, but you've been wearing a frown since Silkie called. The same one that creeps over your features when you talk about the media or having to live in a fishbowl." Indignation bloomed within me when I thought of this life being thrust upon James. "You have no say in it, James, and it isn't fair. I know so many people would kill for fame, but you had no choice."

James smiled, his warm fingers reaching for me, toying with a wisp of hair at my nape. "I've never heard you sound angry before."

"I am angry, James. I'm angry that people you've never met will judge you without knowing the sweet, kind, funny, intelligent man you are. I'm angry that a whole bunch of them will feel some right to be disgusted with you for not being who they think you should be. I'm angry that these strangers get a say in your life. That you're forced to hide who—"

"I'm not forced to hide who I am, Presti. I could walk out the door right now and tell the world I'm gay. I could, but I… It's me. I'm a coward. I'm not ready." James's eyes were devoid of the joy that had been there two hours ago, when he'd been watching me sing, when he'd been talking and laughing with me and Paul, Astrid and Larry. And I hated the world for robbing the happiness of someone who deserved to smile every second of every day.

"There isn't a cowardly bone in your body, James," I replied. My teeth clenched tight as I fought not to blurt out more, as I swallowed down the words to tell James to fight for who he was. Maybe even to fight for me. He would in time, but it had to be in his time.

"Are we ready?" Larry said, tottering toward us uncomfortably in his high heels.

James and I burst out laughing at the sight. I thought it a victory James could laugh at all given the circumstances. "As I'll ever be," he answered.

"Right," Silkie began, "follow my lead and let me do the talking. That sensuous British accent of yours will be our undoing,
Your Highness."

"So will calling him Your Highness, Silkie," I added.

"Quite right. We must have names for you all." Silkie tapped
a thoughtful finger against her full bottom lip.

"Must we?" I asked.

"Oh, indeed. I think for you, sweet boy, we shall have Ana
Conda. Larry will, of course, be Tess Tickles, and for His Highness, we must have Penny Tration."

"No!" Larry, James and I screamed in unison.

Silkie sagged, shook her head as though completely disappointed with us, and then said, "Fine. Let's stick with boring then,
shall we. Scarlet, Rose, and Crimson." Silkie pointed at each of us
in turn, her displeasure showing in her curled lips and snapped
words. I knew she wasn't angry, but Silkie did like to be over the
top. She'd managed that rare skill of living her life unapologetically.

"All right," Astrid said, returning from reconnoitring downstairs. "There are three of them. Each with cameras. I asked them
if they were here to cover the inaugural drag queen class for
F*ckingham Phallus. They fell all over themselves to convince me
they knew James was here. I put on quite the show of ignorance,
I must say."

"Thank you, Astrid," James said.

Astrid nodded. "Right. Let's get you out of here then."

Silkie led the way. We were to follow behind. Nothing but
students obediently following our teacher after a masterclass on

how to successfully 'do drag 'as Silkie insisted. We managed the stairs admirably, descending like angels falling gracefully from heaven, one might say.

Our walk around the side of the building toward the front of the sex shop was more sashay than I'd have thought possible for three men new to the painful world of super high heels.

"Miss Bellbird," a reporter called as we stepped into the open. "Any sign yet of the prince?"

"Shh," Silkie growled. "My students are novices in five-inch heels, so unless you want to foot the exorbitant bill for a nasty fall, do not disturb them. But as you can see we have only baby queens here. No princes."

We kept walking. The scrutiny from the reporters felt thick against my skin as they watched us, eyes narrowed. I held my breath, certain at any moment they'd discover James behind the thick make-up. My pulse thumped as I waited for the flash and glare of their cameras. Surely, they could hear my heart pounding in my chest.

"Look at them," Silkie cooed. "Aren't they sensational? Simply the most divine baby queens I've ever had under my tutelage. Now, if you need a story, that's it. I could do with the free advertising."

Sometimes the uncomfortableness people got around the idea of anything different from societal norms could be a blessing. Their discomfort worked in our favour now as each of the assembled reporters turned away, feigning interest in their equipment or phones. None of them were here for a story on drag queen classes.

"Right, ladies," Silkie went on, undaunted. "Sashay, sashay, and let's add in a flutter, flutter, pop."

Not a single reporter looked our way, their uneasiness increasing. Holy hell, we were going to get away with this.

As long as I live, I'd never forget the sight of James in his ballgown, fluttering and popping. The moon caught on the blue of his eyes even through the giant lashes, his smile swallowing his entire face. Despite possessing a large vocabulary, I couldn't think of a word to accurately describe how glorious he looked. And the sound of his laughter came close to knocking me off my feet.

I could love this boy.

Squashing that dangerous thought as well as I could, I concentrated on not making more of a scene by falling on my arse or — god forbid — kissing the daylights out of James in front of people who desperately wanted to expose every secret he had.

With every step, my confidence increased, but I didn't relax until we'd made it to Silkie's car and were hurtling toward home. James sat quietly in the back, pressed to my side. His fingers entwined with mine, his breath eventually evening out.

"That was too close," he whispered. "I must leave, Presti. I can't—"

"I know, James. I know." And though I understood him not wanting to be found here, I felt sad for him. Sad for us.

Chapter Sixteen

HARLAN ANSWERED IMMEDIATELY, his voice shaky and exhausted. I'd left him holding the bag when I'd fled after those pictures surfaced from our night out in Paris. He'd encouraged me to go and convinced me he understood, but I still felt terrible. The press had more or less left him alone after he'd given his comment that the night out had been his idea. He'd outed himself to save me. He was a better friend than I could ever hope to be.

Abandoning him to take the fall had been the right and wrong thing to do—just like leaving Presti now. My conflicted brain couldn't make sense of anything.

"I'll get you on the first available flight, James," he said quietly once I'd explained the time had come for me to return to the real world. "Are you certain you're ready to come home?" I'd filled him in on my narrow escape tonight, which had led to questions about Presti. Some I hadn't been willing to answer, others I didn't know the answer to.

"How bad has it been?"

"George and Hannah's engagement continues to be the lead story, but our night out and your subsequent disappearance are mentioned daily."

"I'm so sorry, Harlan."

"Nonsense. Nobody cares about me being there that night. They left me alone as soon as I made it clear I would not be commenting further."

"Still, I wish you hadn't been dragged into it." Poor Harlan hated crowds and attention more than I did. His sister's wedding would be a monumental nightmare for him.

"You've managed to avoid the press Down Under, James. Have you been out of doors at all?" Harlan asked. I could hear the click-clack of his keyboard as he planned for my return home while continuing to talk with me.

"Many times. Nobody paid me the slightest bit of attention until tonight." A heavy sigh escaped me. "It was wonderful."

"And this boy…Presti?"

"He's been the best part, Harlan. He…he makes me feel safe. When he's around, I feel like I'm home." Harlan said nothing in response. "Bloody stupid nonsense. Forgive me. I think I've gone a bit bonkers."

"Not at all, James. Sounds like you've found something — someone — special."

"He is. And that's why I need to go. Presti doesn't deserve the shitstorm his life would become if I…well, if I started a relationship with him." Every time I thought about the media blow-up coming my way when I came out, my stomach roiled like a ship tossed in a violent storm. Presti could not be caught up in that nightmare.

"Sounds like it's a little too late for that," Harlan said. "Have you asked him what he wants?"

I shook my head, though Harlan couldn't see me from miles away in merry old England. "It doesn't matter. I won't do that to him."

"You should give him the choice, James. Tell him how you feel and ask him. Don't make decisions for him."

"He won't understand. Not until he's chased down the street by a mob of paparazzi. Not until he finds a photo of himself splashed all over the front pages and realises just how close those zoom lenses can get."

Presti chose that moment to pop his head into the room. I'd barricaded myself in his mother's bedroom as soon as we'd made it home from Paul and Astrid's, excusing myself to make calls. I needed to start extricating myself from the web of feelings that had spun within me. This family I had barged in on only a week ago had sunk their claws into me. And I loved it. The idea of leaving them made me nauseous. Leaving Presti would kill me, so I had to begin pulling away from him while I still had a chance of doing so.

"I'm sorry to interrupt, James," Presti murmured when I waved him in. "I just wanted to see if you needed anything?"

I need you.

The sentiment sat on the tip of my tongue, ready to leap off and out into the world, but I swallowed the words down. I could not be the ruin of this remarkable man. So, instead, I said, "No. Nothing. Thank you."

Presti nodded sadly and left. The sorrow in his eyes gutted me—a sharp pang like a knife to my heart. How badly had I already hurt him?

"Harlan, I need to go. Can you text me the flight details?"

"Of course. Be safe, James."

After thanking Harlan again for his help, I ended the call and walked out to find Presti. He wasn't hard to locate. Already, I knew where he went to feel better.

He stood under the moonlight, surrounded by his beloved plants, looking for all the world like an ethereal being sent to earth to torment me and fill me with joy simultaneously. Pleasure and pain. A temptation I had to be strong enough to resist, or I would destroy the very person I wanted to protect most.

For long seconds, I stood there watching him. He tilted his face toward the light, his eyes closed, his arms stretched out to the side, fingers drifting over the leaves of plants I didn't know the name of as if touching them kept him grounded to this earth. Every so often, he sighed and licked his full bottom lip. He swayed slightly from side to side. He might have been in a trance, but I knew he was calming himself. How well I knew him after so short a time! Presti hid nothing of himself from me.

Every cell in my body stretched toward him, urging me to take him in my arms, hold him tight, and keep him safe. But the best way I could do that was to leave him. I had to go back to the other side of the world, back to my life so far from his.

"I know you have to go, James," he whispered. "But I wish you didn't."

"If I stay… I can't stay, Presti."

He stood side-on to me, his eyes remaining closed. "I know."

Leaving was the right thing, but it felt like the worst, most terrible thing I'd ever do.

"James?"

"Yes?"

Finally, Presti opened his eyes and turned to face me. The blue of his eyes looked silver in the moonlight; his pale skin appeared even whiter against the ink black of his hair. "I know you can't stay. I know I'm not worth it, but would you…stay with me tonight? Just this one night."

Jesus.

"Not worth it? Presti, don't you know?"

"Know what?"

Knots twisted my guts. There was so much I wanted to say. I wanted to scream that he was worth it, that he was worth cutting my heart in two by walking away from him so I could save him. I wanted to shout and yell that I'd stay with him forever if I had my choice. Swear to him that I'd never leave him if staying wouldn't be the ruin of him.

Instead, I stepped closer, the soft scent of alpine I'd forever associate with him tickling my nose. His warmth radiated out, heating the tips of my fingers as I gently traced his brow, down his soft cheek, across his plump lips. "I'm leaving because you're worth everything to me."

My entire body yearned for the feel of him under my hands, against my body. The fear I might never hold him in my arms again after tonight stabbed deep and sharp, an agony dulled only by the thought we'd have tonight. Memories of the perfect man for me were all I'd have left soon.

It wasn't enough.

It would never be enough.

"Presti," I whispered as he turned into my arms, pulled me close, and kissed my lips.

"Please," he moaned, pressing closer, yet still not close enough. He took my hand and led me to his room.

"I've never done this before," Presti murmured as he dropped my hand, reaching for the hem of his T-shirt.

Part of me wanted to still his hand, tell him to save himself for someone worthy, someone who could give him the world. Someone who could give him more than just this one night. But I was a selfish bastard and wanted this memory to hold onto. I wanted memories to keep me warm in the cold, lonely nights I knew would make up the rest of my life. How could I ever walk in the light again once I turned my back on the bright, shining being that was Prestidigitation Jones?

So, I watched him remove his clothes; I gasped at his beauty and melted into his touch. I burned scorching hot as we made love and soared all the way to the heavens.

And when the light of dawn woke me from my dream, I knew I loved him. Because how else could I bear to walk away from this pleasure, this home I'd found with him, if it wasn't the only way I could save him from the nightmare if I stayed?

*

LEAVING PRESTI HURT more than I thought was possible to bear. Undoubtedly, the pain of it should kill me. The flight home to England lasted an eternity, interspersed with memories that drew a blush to my cheeks: the feel of his skin against mine, his soft gasps, the way he pulled me closer in the middle of the night, wanting more.

All I could think about as I sat outside my father's office was Presti. The only place I wanted to be was thousands of kilometres away in an insignificant little house surrounded by a well-loved garden. Presti's bedroom couldn't have been bigger than this little anteroom I sat in now, waiting to feel my father's wrath—worse, my grandmother's. Yet I'd never felt so comfortable, so…*me* in all the rooms of all the palaces as I had in Presti's small room.

"Haven't seen him yet, old boy?" George slapped me on the back as he dropped beside me onto the couch.

"Nope," I muttered. I could hardly meet my brother's eyes. Though I knew he wanted to marry Hannah, I also knew he'd been rushed into it thanks to the mess I'd made.

"Are we planning a big outing?"

Ugh. My brother, about as subtle as a sledgehammer. "No."

"No?" George looked perplexed, which I understood. "I thought… Well, you've kind of got one foot out already, James. Makes sense to just roll with it."

"I'm not ready, George."

George watched me closely, something that looked an awful lot like disappointment in his eyes. I couldn't help that. I had to come out when the time was right for me. "Well," my brother said, standing and stretching to his full height, "when you are ready, you know I'll have your back. Right?"

"I know. And thank you, George, for taking one for the team and marrying Hannah." I smiled, hoping my joke would lighten the mood.

George snorted. "Yeah, real bloody hardship that—marrying a beautiful girl I love and living happily ever after."

"I hope you get your happy ever after," I replied. "You deserve it."

"You deserve it too, James. Don't you forget that."

I blinked at my brother, surprised by his words. Most of the time, George was a massive jackass, but now and then he showed this side—a softer side, a side that said he did care.

"James," my father called, breaking the spell between George and me.

"Good luck, old boy," George said, smirking. He winked and left me to my fate.

Wearily, I rose to my feet and strode into my father's office. Why did it have to be so hard to be myself? Why was it so exhausting? Or was I making it more complicated than it needed to be? I could come out. I had my family's support; I knew that. But I just… I couldn't face the media storm, the public scrutiny. I was a coward.

"It's good to see you, James," my father said as I sat across from him. Papers, a sizeable leatherbound diary, a laptop, and various other stationery items covered his desk. "You scared us." This last part came out barely a whisper, and I wondered if he'd meant to say it at all.

"I'm sorry. That wasn't my intention," I answered.

"I know." He sighed and rubbed his temples as if warding off a headache. "I know this isn't the life you would have chosen, James. But you are a prince of England. Third in line to the throne. You cannot just flit off when things go wrong for you—"

"Go wrong?" I interrupted. "There were photos of me sandwiched between two guys, sporting an… I mean, clearly turned on. That's not going wrong, Father; that's fucking mortifying."

"Language, James." He sighed again. Was it me that exasperated him so much? More than the massive invasion of my privacy? "It was…embarrassing for you, I'm sure, but we face these things. We don't run."

"When was the last time your erection was plastered all over the news?"

A sharp intake of my father's breath warned me I was treading on thin ice. "Never. Because I don't put myself in a situation where they'd be able to get a photo like that."

"So, I don't get to enjoy myself? Be young and free?" We were on the same merry-go-round we often found ourselves on. Everyone in my family agreed the intrusion of the media and the public interest in our private lives was the heavy price we paid for being born who we were, but how to deal with it was something we couldn't quite manage to agree on.

My parents had tried to make arrangements with the press when George and I were born. They'd give them time and opportunities for photographs, and then we'd be left alone. Needless to say, certain parties in the press didn't hold up their end of the bargain.

"You need to be more careful, James." Father shook his head and rubbed his temple again. "Have you decided to come out?"

"No."

"No, you haven't decided, or no, you're not going to come out?"

"I'm not ready. I can't."

My father nodded, and unlike the disappointment I saw in George's eyes, I swear I saw a flicker of relief in my father's. "Very well. Let's agree to put it off until after the wedding."

"Agreed," I nodded.

"Now, what of this boy in Australia?"

"Presti?"

"Yes. The one you ran to. The one you stayed with. What does he mean to you?"

"A friend." The label tasted bitter and wrong, precisely like the lie it was, but I would protect Presti at all costs. Nobody could know how I felt about him. Nobody could know he meant home to me. Nobody could know I'd tear the world apart for him. Christ knew I'd already torn myself in half for him. I'd left a large part of myself with Prestidigitation Jones in Kincumber, Australia.

"Good. Then, let's also agree you won't run off to him again." My father peered at me over his glasses, testing me, watching for any sign that Presti might become a problem for the monarchy. For as much as my father offered to support me, as ready as he'd been to stand behind me if I'd chosen to come out publicly, I didn't believe he was ready for a boyfriend in the bargain. Because that would make it all too real.

"We are friends, Father. Nothing more. And the only contact we shall have from now on is as pen pals."

"Pen pals?"

"Yes."

"Very well. But remember, James, nothing in the letters you exchange that could come back and bite us in the arse." My father nodded and looked down at the papers on his desk, signalling our little tete-a-tete was over.

"I know, Father. I know the rules." I'd been raised on the idea of not trusting anybody outside our immediate family and small circle of close friends. I'd been warned repeatedly about the risks. The consequences of trusting the wrong person had been drilled into me from birth — another thing to hate about life as a royal. Genuine relationships could not be built without trust, and I was conditioned to mistrust.

Without another word, I left.

The palace felt as cold and lonely as it always did as I returned to my rooms. None of the spaces held any warmth, no feeling of home or comfort, even though I'd lived here all my life. I didn't even get to choose my furniture. Instead, I had heirlooms that could have come from a museum. The artworks decorating the walls had hung there for over a century and certainly weren't to my taste. These rooms were for my use, but nothing of me was in them.

Walking to the large window, I looked out at the crowds gathered. It suddenly dawned on me that my home was a tourist attraction. How had I never thought that before? It wasn't lost on me that the people outside looking in would probably give their eye teeth to live behind these walls. They wouldn't understand that I'd swap this entire palace for a small cottage in the tiny, oddly named town of Kincumber any day of the week.

Tired of myself and my whining for one day, I sat down and wrote to Presti. Though I held a lot back, I shared more with him than I dared with any other. Presti knew me, but I wanted him to know more. But he could never know the whole truth. He could never know I loved him.

My letter ended up eight pages long, front and back — a lot, yet not enough. But there'd be more letters because I was selfish and couldn't cut ties with him entirely.

Even as I tucked it in the envelope and sealed my words, I

wondered if he'd write back. Maybe he'd want nothing more to do with me. He'd said he understood I couldn't stay, but we'd had sex, and I still left him. I had been his first lover, and I'd left him the next day. Would he hate me once he'd thought about it? When the dust settled, and I wasn't there, would he resent me? I hated that thought more than anything — except for the idea of his next lover.

Would the throbbing ache of his loss ever ease?

"James?"

"Come in, Hannah," I called, thankful for a reprieve from my indulgent brooding.

My future sister-in-law looked beautiful. She always did, but since her engagement, she glowed. Is that what finding your soulmate did to you? Would I ever glow?

Hannah hugged me as soon as I stood to greet her. She felt small and soft in my arms, everything I thought men wanted in a woman, but I missed the solid bulk of Presti.

"God. You look just awful, James. I'm sorry, but it had to be said."

"Thanks," I scoffed.

Hannah gave me a sad smile and cupped my cheek. "I know we're not brother and sister yet, but I feel somebody has to say this to you."

"What?" I asked, terrified of what was about to come out.

"You are more than a prince, James. You deserve to be happy, to be who you are. And if that upsets the old stiffs in the palace or the homophobes out there, who cares? Harlan, George, and I will fight them all for you if we have to."

Hannah stood a foot shorter than me, yet she possessed a

fierceness that I never wanted to be on the wrong side of.

When I said nothing, she continued, "George told me you weren't ready to come out, and that's okay. Everything in your time, but know that we will not leave you hanging when you're ready."

"Thank you, Hannah. I appreciate it; I do. I just… I'm not ready." Everybody told me to come out in my time when I was ready, yet I felt shame at my cowardice.

"You'll receive a plus-one invitation for my wedding, James. I do hope you use it."

"Thanks," I managed to choke out. My family supported me, and that should be enough. Maybe if I weren't a prince of England, it would be. But it wasn't just family and friends I had to come out to. It was the whole damn world.

Chapter Seventeen

HOW COULD I miss somebody who'd been in my life for such a short period of time?

Saying goodbye to James had been one of the hardest things I'd ever done—and I'd once had to tell Astrid that Larry, though nice to look at, wasn't the most handsome man on the planet. That title could not be claimed until Harrison Ford left this mortal coil—at least, that had been my opinion at the time. Now, poor Harrison had been bumped down a spot, and I would never remind Astrid that meant poor Larry was number three.

Though our farewell was brutal, we'd done it. James and I had shared a private goodbye at home and then a public, no-touching goodbye at the airport. I'd been fascinated to learn that James had an ordinary passport in the name of James Wales as well as his royal one.

He'd travelled to Australia and back to England as plain

Jimmy Wales, he'd said. If anybody at the airport recognised him, they'd kept it to themselves. Fortunately, royalty didn't hold quite the fascination for the general public here in Australia that it did in England.

He'd been gone a week. He'd called me twice; I'd called him. I'd received a letter and was in the process of replying to him. He'd told me he'd threatened Simon de-fucking-Montfort with beheading if he interfered with our correspondence again. His forcefulness in fighting for our penpalship fanned the flames of desire. I only wish I'd been there to see James in action.

Things between us were…friendly. We were friends. He hadn't mentioned anything more, and neither had I.

How could there be more?

I'd been a ninny to even to entertain the idea of James and I becoming a couple. Ugh, I amazed myself with my foolishness sometimes.

"Presti?"

"Yes, Mum?"

"I'm making lasagne for dinner. Would you like to help?"

"Sure."

My mum watched me from the door of my room, her light eyes considering, not missing a thing. "When I first met your father, I thought we'd be together forever."

"Is this a life lesson, Mum? I think I've always been quite realistic about James and me."

"Yes. You have. But that's not what I mean." Mum came into my room and sat beside me on my bed. "You've never allowed yourself to believe in you and James. And I get that. Protecting your heart and all that."

I wasn't sure what Mum was trying to say, but I'd listen to her about anything because I trusted no one more than her.

"When I first got together with your father, I dreamed of weddings and babies, making a home and a family. A fantasy life. I got the baby, but none of the other stuff."

"So, I'm doing the right thing by not hoping for more from James?"

"Oh, honey, your father never once looked at me the way James looks at you. All I'm saying is that if he should ask for more from you, don't be afraid to give it." Mum sighed and patted my knee. "If I'd have kept my heart locked away after your father broke it, I wouldn't have Howard in my life. And what a great tragedy that would be."

"So, you're saying I should leave my heart open to be hurt?"

"Exactly." Mum sprang up from the bed and moved toward the door. "What are we here for if not for love?"

Penelope Jones. My mother. Hopeless romantic.

Mum didn't mention James again the entire time we made lasagne. We talked of plants, people we knew, and even the state of the world — a topic we generally steered clear of because we found it too depressing. We laughed. We made memories of another night, just the two of us, being a family.

As we washed the dishes, the sharp trill of my phone broke the harmony. "Royals" by Lorde. The ringtone I'd chosen for James.

"Well, well," my mother smirked. "Speak of the devil." Tossing the tea towel on the bench, she pinched my cheek and left the room.

"Hello," I answered before she'd cleared the door trim.

"Hello, Presti."

"It's good to hear your voice, James. Is everything going well?" I launched onto the kitchen bench, kicking my feet like a little kid about to get his favourite treat.

"Lots and lots of wedding stuff. I had no idea there was so much to it."

"Flowers and suits and dresses, oh my."

James laughed his beautiful laugh. "Dinner settings and invite lists and vows, oh my."

"Is Hannah managing?" We'd spoken about his brother's betrothed. James had been adamant she was strong enough to handle the task of marrying the future king, but I couldn't begin to imagine the pressure.

"Hannah is doing great. Mum throws ideas out there, and Hannah… Well, she picks her battles. All she wants is to marry George. She is firm on a few things though."

"Such as?"

For a moment, James stayed quiet. I wondered if I'd lost him, and then he said, "The guest list for one. That is why I've called."

"For the guest list?"

"Yes."

"I see." I didn't see at all.

"Hannah insists I bring a plus-one to the wedding, and I" — James hauled in a deep breath — "I would very much like for you to be my plus-one, Presti."

"Me?"

"Yes."

"Your date?"

"Yes."

"To the royal wedding of the century?" *Was I dreaming*? "In public? Before god and everyone?"

"Yes." A heavy sigh from James settled into the silence. "I understand this is asking a lot of you, Presti. There'll be substantial interest in you. If you think it's too much—"

"Yes," I exclaimed.

"Yes, it's too much?"

Oh god, I was making a dreadful horlicks of this. "No. The other one. Yes, to going as your plus-one."

"Really? It's not too much?"

"James, you've asked me to attend your brother's wedding as your plus-one. That's all." I could not wipe the ridiculous grin off my face.

"It's not an average wedding, Presti. The entire world will be watching."

"That's a little conceited, isn't it?" I teased. "A good portion of the world will be watching certainly, but not the entire world. Some people have no TVs, and others think your family are lizard aliens running some kind of slave trade on our planet. And, of course, some people are just not interested."

"You make excellent points, Presti. But do tell me more about us being aliens. I don't think I've heard that one." James's warm laugh tickled my ear.

"Will you be making an announcement before the wedding?"

"You mean, will I be coming out before you and I set the world on fire?"

"Mm." James dating a man would be a huge deal, regardless

of how we'd progressed as a civilisation. Far too many still thought it was their business who other people loved.

"Well, I kind of thought having you as my date would speak for itself," James mumbled. His hesitation warned me he hadn't thought this through. Something had compelled him to call and ask me to his brother's wedding, yet I knew another something could just as easily change his mind.

No matter how much he wanted to be, I didn't believe James was ready to be out, at least not in front of the entire world. Honestly, the idea gave me pause. I hadn't cared what people thought of my sexuality for a long time.

Though I doubted James's commitment to this plan, the joy I felt that he'd asked me was immeasurable.

"Presti," James said. "There's never been anybody I've been willing to come out for. Not until you. I wish I could promise you that I… Well, I hope I don't…"

"I know, James. And if you can't do it, it's okay."

Was it possible to be so happy? I'd have thought not, but here I was, feeling as if I might burst with all the joy inside me.

Naturally, it was not to last.

Less than two weeks later, James sent me a perfectly reasonable letter explaining the many reasons he had to withdraw his invitation. It was nothing personal, he explained. A simple change of mind. It turns out I was right, and he wasn't ready to come out at all, which, in effect, ended the possibility of me being his date to Prince George's wedding.

I understood. I did. Yet, that didn't ease the ache in my breastbone.

Chapter Eighteen

AS IT TURNED out, Presti didn't hate me even after I withdrew his invitation to George's wedding. I hated myself enough for both of us though. What a coward I was. After two weeks of almost constant panic about Presti as my date, I'd finally chickened out. And worse, I'd done it by mail. George and Hannah hadn't said much when I'd told them, but I saw the look they gave me as if I was the greatest ball-less wonder they'd ever known. I'd expected comments or digs over my lack of spine, but their quiet disappointment felt worse.

Presti had written back immediately. A generous letter expunging me of any blame — words of forgiveness and understanding that I didn't deserve.

If I possessed any decency, I should have ended things right then with Presti. But it seemed not only was I a coward, but selfishness was also another grand trait I could claim. I couldn't let him go. I couldn't say goodbye to him—couldn't even write it. So, we continued our penpalship for months. We wrote weekly, and once or twice, we'd spoken on the phone, usually when one of us—most often me—had too much to drink.

With every word he shared on the page, I came to know him better and miss him more. I'd never told anybody the things I admitted to Presti. Oddly, I knew the danger of doing so but couldn't stop myself. If our letters became public, I didn't know if I could bounce back from the shame. His last letter had arrived yesterday, and I'd devoured it as I had all of the others, but writing back would have to wait.

George's wedding day dawned, the sky a perfect blue as I knew it would be. The universe would never dare rain on George and Hannah's fairy tale. Presti's letter caught my eye where it lay on my side table as I ran a comb through my drying hair. My fingers itched to re-read his words, but royal weddings never ran late. Every minute of the day must be timed to perfection. Heads would roll if the wedding did not go off without a hitch.

At precisely eleven a.m., I needed to be standing at George's side in Westminster Abbey, turned out in my military attire despite never actually serving. Even now, hundreds of people were polishing buttons, sprucing floral decorations, and steaming seams to within an inch of their lives. We must look, act, and *be* perfect.

I felt sick.

"James!" George shouted as he ran into my room, followed closely by a far less buoyant Harlan. "It's here. Today's the day."

Credit to my brother, despite not being fully mature, he was honestly happy to be marrying Hannah.

"Poor Hannah," I said with a smile. "Do you think she's trying to climb out the window right now?"

George snorted. "Not bloody likely. How many girls would turn down being a princess?"

"More than you'd think," I murmured. George thought being royalty was the best. He loved his life and loved the thought of being king one day. And that was a good thing because what choice did he have? Even less than I did.

"Well, none of them would turn down having me as a husband, royal or not," George answered.

"You're a nincompoop." I laughed. Nothing would dampen George's spirits today, and I'd do my best not even to try.

"Hard to believe this nincompoop will be king one day," George smirked, looked down at himself, and ran his palms down his chest. Though he wore his uniform, he hadn't added the medals yet. "I am one fine-looking nincompoop, though."

The only answer I had for him was a roll of my eyes. "So, clearly, you're feeling okay about today, George. How're you doing, Harlan?"

Harlan, usually pale, was an even whiter shade today. His wide eyes looked startled as if he couldn't believe today was happening. "Oh, fine," he answered. "I don't have that big of a starring role. Hopefully, no one will be paying me any attention at all."

George snorted. "Of course, they won't. Not when there's me to look at."

"Oh boy," Harlan sighed. "I hope Hannah has thought this through."

I hoped she had too. Marrying into royalty could be—was

likely to be — a huge burden, more pressure than most newlyweds had to endure. But if anybody could do it, Hannah could.

An hour and a half later, as I watched her walk down the aisle toward my waiting brother, I knew I was right. Hannah looked radiant, her smile beaming out from beneath her veil. She hadn't put a foot wrong, her poise and grace carrying her through what had to be a nerve-wracking day. Any bride would be anxious, but to be married before a television audience of possibly billions… Now, that was some nerve-inducing stuff.

They managed their vows effortlessly. I wondered if it was because they knew, deep in their souls, that they were marrying the right person. Would that ever be me? Would I ever stand beside my soulmate and promise them forever before god, king, and country? Hell, in my case, the entire world?

Thoughts like that dragged Presti into my consciousness. Over the past six months, I'd gotten good at pushing him from my thoughts. Times when I read his letters or wrote my own to him, he was at the forefront of my thoughts. In those moments, I recalled every second of our time together, every touch. Hell, some days, I even thought I could smell him or feel the softness and warmth of his skin. But with those memories came the pain of our separation, the shame of my rescinded invite. I had treated Presti appallingly, yet he'd managed to forgive me. I wanted him so much that I ruthlessly shoved him in a box and locked away those memories as much as I could because to do otherwise hurt too much.

Despite throwing myself into my royal duties, the pain of being separated from Presti never dulled. The ache of loss in my chest never eased.

As I filed out of Westminster Abbey behind my newlywed brother and sister-in-law, my traitorous brain couldn't help imagining me and my husband in their position. A vision of us holding hands and looking as happy as George and Hannah as we faced the public for the first time as husband and husband.

And that husband of my imagination looked suspiciously like one Prestidigitation Jones.

Dammit.

Chapter Nineteen

PRESTIDIGITATION JONES!" ASTRID cried. "Please tell me you are not watching that wedding again!"

"Nope," I shouted, far too loudly and defensively to be believed.

Astrid prowled into the room, rounded the armchair, and glared at the television screen. The one with a frozen image of Prince James at his brother's wedding, all dressed up and looking more spectacular than any man had a right to.

"So, you've sunk to lying to me now? I never would have thought this of you."

Putting a little something extra into my sigh, I looked at my best friend. "It's just easier. Saves me from one of your lectures."

Astrid perched on the coffee table, blocking my view of frozen James. "I lecture because I care, Pres. It's been six months. No, almost seven now since he departed our shores."

"I know."

"And he hasn't come back," she added sadly.

"I know."

"He uninvited you as his plus-one." Astrid, unlike me, had fumed over James rescinding his invitation. I'd been angry for a millisecond but understood James's reasonings.

Astrid's anger had eased. Mostly.

"I hate seeing you like this."

"I am perfectly well, Astrid," I lied. While James and I were in a penpalship, I missed his actual presence. I missed feeling his warm skin or watching a crooked smile play over his features. I missed how he'd nibble on his lip when thinking or the crinkle around his eyes when he smiled. He'd only stayed here a week but changed everything for me.

Our correspondence, though a lifeline to my sanity, was not enough. I was a walking, talking example of not knowing what you had until you lost it. And I'd lost James. He wasn't ready to come out, and I would never pressure him. But was I going to wait for him to be ready? Would he even want me to wait? There was a greater-than-average probability that I meant nowhere near as much to him as he did to me.

"Do you not think he looks quite forlorn here?" I asked, my gaze shifting back to the screen and the frozen image of James. He'd smiled plenty on the day. So much that I doubt anybody else noticed, but I'd also caught glimpses of melancholy in James's handsome features that day. Was I imagining I knew him so well after such a short period of time? Astrid and Larry practically finished each other's sentences after they'd been together only three weeks. Now, they indulged in silent conversations, reading each other so well they didn't need to speak. I wanted that. I wanted to feel that connection with another. I wanted to look at somebody and know what they were thinking. I wanted to be somebody's world.

James and I might have had that in an alternate universe, but his regality seemed insurmountable.

"Presti, please." Astrid had tried her best to distract me from my obsession with James. She liked him well enough, but…well, I guess she was more of a realist than I was. I was still hoping for some dramatic and romantic gesture from James. Perhaps something with him publicly announcing his undying love for me to the world. Something involving rose petals and, for some obscure reason, fairy floss. Ridiculous. I could be a complete fopdoodle at times.

The truth was that while James liked me well enough, there was nothing more to it than that. I wasn't worth him coming out for. He'd been a dream, a fantasy that I could hold onto for the rest of my life, nothing more. I could bury myself away in that fantasy forever.

Or I could put myself out there and try to find something real with someone who wasn't freaking royalty.

"Astrid, I… I think I should put myself on the Grindr."

"*The* Grindr? Oh boy." Astrid pinched the bridge of her nose, her signs of frustration well known to me. "First of all, it's just Grindr. Second, I thought we had agreed we would not participate in such…social absurdities."

"Well, I can't see myself finding a date any other way. I will not rub produce at the supermarket."

"What?" Astrid asked, a furrow on her brow.

"Silkie's Guide to Picking Up 101."

"Oh."

"Mm. And I need to find a date, Astrid. I must erase the spectre of James from my mind."

"The spectre? He is not a poltergeist. If he were not a prince…things would have been different. You and he… You worked, Presti." Astrid reached and tucked a wayward lock of hair behind my ear.

"Not well enough," I muttered.

"Are you angry with him?"

Was I? "No. Not really. And I understand him not being ready to come out, but… One day, I will have to watch him with another man. I will have to sit and watch him walk down the aisle with someone else. Photos of them will be plastered over every magazine cover. They'll be on every news channel. James and his lover will be shoved down my throat."

"Oh, dear. Quite the imagery." Astrid sighed and leaned closer. "You could wait for him."

"No. No. What if I wait and he still doesn't choose me? I think it best I get out there and sow my oats."

"Well, we can get your oats sown without resorting to Grindr. Perhaps Larry—"

"Presti! My god, Presti, are you home?" The front door slammed open and closed so hard the house shook as my mother barrelled in, shouting for me.

"In here," I yelled back. "Goodness, Mum, what on earth?"

Mum ran into the room, comically skidded to a stop, then bent with her hands on her knees, gasping for breath. "It's…James." She sucked in a deep breath. "Well, no, not James.

His father and brother."

Blood froze in my veins. The tone of my mother's voice, the look of dread in her eyes. What had happened? "Mother?"

"Turn the TV on. It'll be all over the news," she replied, still dragging in large gulps of air and flailing her arms about.

Panic at my mother's distress curdled my insides as I fumbled for the remote. As soon as I pressed Stop, the video of the royal wedding switched off, live television taking its place. A news ticker scrolled along the bottom of the screen. I read the words with a growing sense of dread and disbelief.

Prince Arthur Dead! The ticker screamed. *Prince George Believed to be in Critical Condition!*

Oh my god. "What happened?" I screamed, my hands flying to cover my mouth. *Why did humans do that in times of trauma?* Perhaps it was a vain effort to hold a scream in or swallow it down. And what a stupid thought to be having at such a time.

"Helicopter crash," my mother exclaimed, still quite breathless. "They were on their way to some engagement and…" She flailed her hands about again.

"James," I gasped.

"No. He wasn't there."

Relief flooded through me like a tidal wave — my icy blood thawing. James was safe, but his family. Oh, he'd lost his father and might lose his brother. I ached to be there with him, to hold him in my arms, as weak as they were. Nothing I could do for James would be of any help, and I must be the last thing on his mind right now, yet I felt this overwhelming sense that I needed to be there for him. That he needed me.

"What should I do? What can I do?" I half screamed,

panicked and desperate to be with James, to help him heal.

"I'm not certain you can do anything, Presti. I can only imagine the ranks closing around the royal family right now." My mother kissed the top of my head and gently squeezed my hand. "Poor, poor James."

Despite losing my grandfather and friends I'd made at the Home Strait, I'd never lost a parent. Of course, I'd only ever had one—my mother—and I could not even begin to fathom the trauma of losing her. From my understanding, James wasn't as close with his father as I was with her, but still…

My stomach lurched uncomfortably as I pondered James's suffering, my reaction to his tragic news quite visceral. I'd give everything I owned to be there with him now. Not that I owned much, but even if I owned the world, I'd give it all up for him.

"Presti? Are you okay?" Astrid asked softly.

"Huh?"

"Silly question, I know, but needed to be asked."

"I don't think I'm okay at all. I feel… Remember when Mr Eustace told us his dying wish was one last dance with Mrs Eustace?"

"Quite. Poor chap had quite forgotten Mrs Eustace had passed three months previous."

"Exactly. Multiply our feeling of helplessness that day by about three quadrillion, and that's how I feel."

"Oh, Presti," Mum murmured.

"And sad, Mum. I feel so desperately sad for James, and there isn't a damn thing I can do to help him. How can I fix this?"

"This isn't something you can fix, Presti. All you can do is be there for him. Call him."

"Do you think he'll want me to disturb him at a time like this?"

"Presti, honey," my mum whispered, brushing my hair out of my eyes. "I don't know everything that happened between you and James, but I saw you together the day he left, so I know, if nothing else, that the two of you are friends. If now is not a time to prove your friendship, then I don't know when is."

"Perhaps I should—"

"Presti, your mother is right. Call James. Make sure he knows he has at least one true friend to count on during this terrible time."

They were right—both of them. I had to put aside any doubt or fear of rejection. This wasn't about me. This was everything about James. My poor, soft-hearted James. Now I just had to decide what to say to him.

If he even answered the phone.

Ugh. The angst threatened to overwhelm me. But the memory of my time with James, the gentle touches, the soft-spoken words. He had to know I was here for him, whatever he needed at this awful time. I had to ensure he knew I was thinking of him and was there for him even from ten thousand kilometres away.

"Okay. Okay, I'll do it. Give me the phone." Mum and Astrid stared at me until I realised my phone was in the back pocket of my jeans. "Oh, right."

As I punched a finger at my phone, I paced the room, my entire body vibrating with nervous energy and bone-deep sorrow. *James. Oh, James.*

"Presti," a soft, shaken voice answered.

"James?" I asked, somewhat unsure. The voice sounded like James's, but it was a broken version of the happy voice I remembered.

"It's me."

"James." I sighed. "I'm so very sorry."

"Thank you." His tone was stiff, lifeless. No doubt I wasn't the first person to express my sympathy to him.

"What can I do?" I asked. Right then, I thought I might try to fly to the moon for him if that's what he said he needed.

"I don't know. God, Presti, I feel so lost. Mum… Well, she's devastated, and poor Hannah… And Gran, well, she has to… We all must keep the stiff upper lip." James sounded so ragged, so torn apart between the twin burden of grief and duty.

"Not with me, James. You don't need to pretend with me."

For a few short moments, I got nothing but silence and then came quiet sobbing. My heart tore clear in two as I listened to James's wretched grief. "James," I whispered over and over. The frustration of not being able to hold him in my arms felt fierce enough to kill me. Impotent rage at the distance between us, the unfairness of such a tragedy visiting someone as good as James burned through my veins. Life could be cruel. No more valid words were ever uttered.

"I'm sorry," James hiccupped. "I didn't mean to fall apart like that."

"Is that the first time you've cried since…"

"Yes."

Jesus. My heart shattered anew for this poor boy. At some point, Mum and Astrid had quietly slipped from the room. Though I appreciated the gesture of privacy, I wished they were still there with me. I didn't know how to fix James.

"James," I murmured. "I don't know what to say. I don't know how to help you, and I'm so far away. I'd give anything to be able to hold you through this."

"That helps, Presti. Those words help."

"How is George? Is there any…news?" God, I wanted him to tell me George was awake, walking and talking. It wouldn't make up for the loss of his father, but it'd be some relief.

"The best the doctors can give us is that he has a chance if he makes it through the night. And even if he does, they don't know… There's a good chance he'll never be the same again."

What does one say to that? I was so out of my depth. But there was no way in hell I'd turn my back on him.

"What can I do? Anything, James," I begged, desperate for him to give me a task and tell me what to do to help him.

There was more silence for a moment, and I wondered if I'd overstepped. And then came James's soft, heart-sore voice: "You, Presti. I only need you…this. Your voice, knowing you're there for me. It helps."

"I'll be here no matter what. If you want me there, I'll jump on a plane. If you just need to talk, I'll listen. Whatever it is you need from me, it's yours."

A tiny, sad half laugh came before James said, "I'm so tired, but I can't sleep. The doctor gave me something to help, but I didn't want to take anything. I wish… The best sleep I ever had was in your bed, in your arms. I wish I were there now, Presti."

"I wish you were, too, but for now, go and hop into bed. I'll stay with you on the phone until you fall asleep, James."

A lot of rustling sounded over the line as I listened to James shuffle around his room. By my reckoning, it was the early morning hours over there. Even if James slept now, I suspected it would be a broken sleep, and he'd be woken early to do his…princely duty at this terrible time.

"You know the worst thing?" James suddenly whispered.

I couldn't even begin to imagine. "What?" I whispered back.

"When they called me in to tell me, Simon was there, and I overheard him talking about the line of succession, and now, well, I keep thinking that this—what happened to Dad and George—it might mean I'm king one day. How selfish is that? How can I even be thinking about that now?"

How could the people around him worry about the line of succession rather than be concerned about James? That's what I wanted to know. That's what I wanted to scream and rant about. How could they not be putting James's welfare first?

"There is no right or wrong way to grieve, James. Everything you're feeling is valid. It's okay to be thinking about everything."

"I never wanted this life," James continued. "Being royal, rich…famous. I never wanted any of it. And I know that makes me sound like a spoiled little rich kid, but it's true. I've only ever wanted a simple life. I can't be king, Pres. I just can't. I'm so tired. I…"

Jesus. "Shh now, James. Let's worry about that later. Close your eyes. I'll stay with you."

"Tell me about Kincumber, Pres. Tell me about your garden and your mum. Tell me about Astrid, Paul, and Larry. Tell me about everyone at the Home Strait."

And so, I did. I spoke for an hour or more. I kept talking even after I heard James's soft snores. I told him how much I missed him. How much we all missed him. I told him about the fantasies I only allowed myself in the small hours of the night of him and me together. A real life. A happy life. I told him I'd do anything for him. I told him I'd burn the world down if it would take away his pain.

I told him I loved him.

Chapter Twenty

PRESTI LOVED ME.

Had he meant to tell me that? Had he meant for me to hear those words? Had I dreamt them? He loved me, and I loved him. It should be as simple as that, but it wasn't. That much I knew. I couldn't, shouldn't, even be thinking about this now.

My father was dead.

Dead.

I'd whispered the words a thousand times since it happened, let them roll around in my mind, and I still couldn't believe them. The last day had to be a nightmare. I so desperately wanted my father's death and my brother's injuries to be nothing more than a terrible dream. But I knew they weren't. A terrible pain had taken root inside me. A grief that I didn't know how to deal with.

Four years ago, I'd lost my grandfather. And that was it.

That was the total loss I'd experienced in my life. I'd been lucky in so many ways.

How was I going to get through this? And how was I supposed to do it alone?

Every cell in my body screamed as though I was being torn apart. Duty and family loyalty pulled me in one direction. But from thousands of kilometres away, Presti's warmth and love pulled me in another.

Though soft, the knock on my door echoed like a drumbeat in my foggy brain. Nothing seemed real. Perhaps I was in a dream, a nightmare that I was having a damn hard time waking from.

"Come in," I called.

Simon de-fucking-Montfort skulked into my rooms, looking pristine, polished and too fucking put together for someone who should be grieving the loss of his beloved future king. "The queen wishes to see you, James."

"What does my grandmother want?" I asked rather spitefully. I hated this guy and all he represented. Simon de Montfort didn't see any of us as people. We were part of the establishment to be maneuvered and used as our courtiers saw fit.

"There are plans to be discussed, James. The princes 'vigil at your father's coffin, a walkabout with the mourning public —"

"You expect me to go out there, shake hands, and smile for strangers mourning my father? No. Absolutely not. The vigil I can do as respect for my father, but the walkabout…NO!" I shook my head just to put an exclamation mark on my unwillingness. Did the public expect me to go out there and accept their condolences days after losing my father? And while my brother's life still hung in the balance?

Impossible.

"I think you'll find that's exactly what Her Majesty expects of you, James. This country has lost its future king—"

"I've lost my fucking *father*," I raged. "What does my mother have to say about this?"

My mother was at the hospital with my brother after her flight home from the Caribbean, where she'd been on royal duties when the accident occurred. She surely did not want me to do this. She would come and wrap me in her arms, under her maternal protection, during this awful time. That's what I expected of my mother.

"Your mother intends to join you on the walkabout," Simon replied, leaving me thoroughly agog.

"I don't believe you." I stormed past Simon, accidentally knocking into him as I went. Damn, it felt good when I almost put him on his arse.

The palace halls were quiet, except for my pounding feet as I strode toward my grandmother's office. She'd be in there, eighty-one years old, and rather than mourning her son, I knew she'd be working, trying to save the monarchy from my father's loss.

Ignoring twenty-odd years of indoctrinated protocol, I opened her door and entered uninvited. "Granny, I'm not doing it."

Her Majesty looked at me over the rim of her glasses, displeasure rather than grief etching the lines of her forehead and colouring her hazel eyes. "James. Do come in."

Chastised, I entered the office and closed the door behind

me, leaving Simon de Montfort on the other side. "I can't do it, Gran. The walkabout. All those people watching me, wanting *me* to give *them* comfort. I can't. I have nothing to give. He was my father."

"And he was their future king," came her response. "Sit down, James."

I watched her face, searching for a hint of a grandmother comforting her grandson over his terrible loss. All I could find was duty and stoic acceptance.

"This is a difficult time, James. I know that. I've lost my own father. I know how it hurts, but our lives aren't our own; our grief is not private. We belong to our people. It's the price we pay."

"I don't believe that, Gran. I don't believe the people expect us to get out there and accept flowers and handshakes when we've just lost someone…when I've just lost my father." Tears pricked at my eyes, but I knew tears in the queen's presence were… Well, it wasn't how things were done.

"It is exactly what they expect. It'll only be for a short time. Hannah and your mother will be with you —"

"Hannah? No. No way. You cannot ask that of her. She's a new bride, her husband might yet die, and she's…she's pregnant. She could lose the baby."

Only a handful knew of Hannah's pregnancy. She'd been pregnant at the wedding, and Gran wanted to do everything she could to prevent people from finding out. A pushed-out due date would be given when the pregnancy was eventually announced, and then, of course, she'd go into labour *early* when the time came. It simply wouldn't do for the public to know there'd been a 'shotgun 'wedding for the second in line to the throne.

No.

He was now the first in line to the throne.

"Hannah will do her duty, as must you, James. She will need you there."

And there was the manipulation I knew would eventually spawn its ugliness. I hadn't known where it would come from, but I knew there'd be something the queen and Simon would have up their sleeves to get me to toe the line. There always was.

"When is it to be?" I asked, defeated. I'd never let Hannah go out there alone.

"Your mother returns in two hours. The walkabout is planned for this afternoon. Sufficient floral tributes have built up, and a substantial crowd still ambles about the palace gates to make a success of it. I'll do my walkabout tomorrow with your uncles, John and Albert."

Make a success of it. We weren't talking about a garden party, for Christ's sake.

"And the Vigil of the Princes?"

"Two days from now. Queues are already forming to file past your father's coffin."

The coldness, the businesslike way my grandmother was discussing her son's death appalled me and turned my stomach to acid. I'd always admired my grandmother's sense of duty and work ethic, but this was too much. I needed to get the hell away from her before I said something I couldn't ever take back.

"I'll be ready," I muttered and fled, ignoring the smug look on Simon de-fucking Montfort's face as I blew by him in a blur of frustrated anger and bone-deep sorrow.

"Harlan, are you busy?" I asked without preamble when

Harlan answered my call after I returned to my room.

"Just saw poor Hannah off to sleep," Harlan replied. "Poor sparrow finally crashed with exhaustion. She won't take anything, not with her being…well, with child, and she hasn't slept a wink since—"

"Are you still at the palace?"

"Yes. What can I do, James?"

"Could you pop by my rooms? I need… Well, I'm not certain what I need except to not be alone with my bloody thoughts."

"On my way," Harlan answered and ended the call.

He wasn't the man I wanted—needed—but he was a damn sight better than the cold nothingness of my grandmother. I'd never have dragged him from his sister's side, but I'd borrow him for a few minutes while she slept.

George and Hannah's rooms were down the hall, so Harlan's knock came in moments. He looked almost as wrecked as I knew I must.

"Well, you look bloody awful, James," he said, voicing my thoughts. "To be expected." Harlan embraced me, his slight body belying the strength of his hug.

"How's Hannah?" I asked. "Stupid bloody question."

"She's holding it together. I um…" Harlan looked about, his gaze landing everywhere but on mine.

"What is it, Harlan?"

He sighed and finally met my eyes. "I'm not happy about this bloody walkabout, James."

"Me neither. I've tried to talk Gran out of it, but… If Hannah isn't up to it, Harlan, tell her to stay in her rooms."

"That's just it, James. Hannah insists she must do it. Wants

George to be proud of her when he wakes up."

"Jesus," I murmured and dropped into my favourite chair.

"Anyway, I told her I'll be with her if she must do it." Harlan sighed, ran his fingers through his messy hair and sank into the armchair opposite mine.

"Good," I sighed. "We'll both be there for her."

"And you, James. We'll be there for you too."

This wasn't the first time Harlan would have my back. Yet, he wasn't the one I needed. If I'd dared to show the world who I truly was, I might have had Presti here when I needed him most. But I'd been a coward, and now I was so horribly alone.

"I wish… I wish Presti could be here. I feel so lost."

"Could he not be here? Surely, they would allow it."

They were the queen and her advisors and courtiers. And they would never risk Presti's presence during this time. Though they might be willing to allow me to come out, it would be at a time, place, and in a manner of their choosing.

"I'm afraid not. But they can't stop me from calling him."

Harlan leaned forward and squeezed my knee. "I'm so sorry, James."

"Thank you, Harlan."

"I'll leave you to your call." Harlan left me, returning to his vigil at his sister's side.

I found my phone, curled up in my chair, and called Presti.

He answered on the first ring. "James?"

"Hey."

"Hey. How are you?"

"Angry," I replied.

"At what?"

"My grandmother is making me do a walkabout."

"Sorry?"

"Mum, Hannah, and I are going out to walk amongst the mourners gathered at the palace."

For a moment, Presti said nothing, and then shouted, "What the bloody hell for?"

"To keep up appearances. To be there for our subjects. Take your pick," I snapped. "Shit. I'm sorry, Presti. I shouldn't be taking this out on you."

"James, if you need to yell, you go ahead and yell. You won't scare me off. When my grandfather died, my grandmother yelled at Mungo Phillips for twenty minutes but said she felt much better afterwards. Turned poor Mungo's hair white with the language she used, but she wasn't angry with him. She was furious Pa had left her, even if he was a mean old curmudgeon."

A chuckle slipped out at Presti's words. God, I missed him. "I wish you were here," I whispered.

"James," he whispered back.

"I can't believe he's gone. Do you know that when I was little, Dad used to call me Fanta because I loved the colour orange? Mum wanted me to wear blues and greys, but Dad used to buy me bright-orange shirts and pants."

"I didn't know," Presti said.

"There's some photos of me in some very questionable outfits Dad used to let me get away with that nobody else would have."

"I shall have to do some googling."

Suddenly, the floodgates opened, and I wanted to tell Presti everything I could about my father. "And he used to sneak treats to George and me that the palace chef would have had a heart attack about if he knew."

Presti laughed, so I told him more and more. I spoke to Presti for hours, and before I knew it, there was a knock on my door, and there stood my mother, eyes red-rimmed, her slight body looking even more vulnerable. "Presti, I must go, but thank you for listening."

"I will listen to you whenever you need, James. Please be careful on your walkabout and know I'm thinking of you the whole time."

Grief and gratitude lodged in my throat, and my words choked on the emotions. "Thank you," I murmured, then hung up.

"Mum…" I ran into her arms as soon as I put the phone down. We gripped each other as though we'd fly apart if we were to let go. "Mum."

"Shh, James. I've got you," she whispered.

"I'm so sorry, Mum. So, so sorry."

My mother was a strong woman, and she'd loved my father. Her grief sapped her strength as she sagged in my arms. "Oh, James. I can't believe…"

"I know. I can't believe it either."

"I spoke to him just an hour before."

"Mum," I said and pulled out of her arms. "Tell Gran you don't want to do this walkabout. You shouldn't have to be out there—"

"No, we shouldn't, but if I'm out there putting on a show, then I'm not thinking about what I've lost—what we've lost."

I hadn't thought of it that way and wasn't sure it would

work for me, but if it helped Mum, I'd do it.

A short time later, Hannah, Harlan, my mother, and I did our duty. We smiled ghoulishly at the people when they offered us their condolences. We accepted their flowers, handshakes, and the odd attempt at a hug from small children.

And I was selfishly glad of Hannah's presence because it gave me something to focus on. I was so busy worrying about her that I didn't have time to consider my loss and how I was walking about in front of strangers with my chest torn open and my heart shredded in pieces.

*

THE NEXT FORTY-eight hours felt like I was trying to wade through quicksand. George remained in a coma. Mother was busy with the queen making arrangements for a funeral that had been planned since my father became an adult. All our funerals were planned. Nothing about our lives was spontaneous or left to chance.

Once I'd turned eighteen, I'd been invited to attend a meeting to plan my funeral. My death had been codenamed *London's Eye Stopped Spinning* so it could be spoken about without alerting anyone not in the know until the palace was ready to make an announcement. Unbelievable.

After the torturous walkabout, I'd been left pretty much alone. Presti and I called each other frequently. He often stayed on the line with me, listening as I rambled, or sharing the silence of my grief with me. Though not physically with me, he was the strength keeping my head above the quicksand.

It had been hours now since I'd spoken to him, however. I'd

finally managed some decent sleep, and I knew it would be the middle of the night for him now. He'd stayed awake with me for almost three days, and I wanted to let him sleep.

But I also wanted to hear his voice before I faced the nightmare of the princes' vigil. My uncles, eldest cousins, and I would stand at my father's coffin for one hour as crowds continued to file past, paying their respects to a man they didn't know and who would never be their king now.

Though I'd been to many solemn occasions in my life of public duty, I'd never had to stand still in one position for an hour. Given the flux of my emotions, the roiling in my stomach and my utter exhaustion, I had no idea how I would manage it.

Presti's soothing voice and quiet confidence in me were what I needed.

But I didn't get it.

My fifth and final attempt to call him went unanswered only seconds before I stepped into the hall containing my father's coffin.

Chapter Twenty-One

JAMES MUST HAVE looked like a picture of perfect, stoic poise for the rest of the world. His legs spread slightly, arms at his side, head slightly bowed as he stood silently alongside his father's coffin.

But I noticed a tiny tremble in his otherwise steady limbs, the occasional hitch in his breathing, the almost translucent paleness of his skin. He might appear unshakeable on the outside, but James was crumbling on the inside.

Every cell in my body begged to go to him, wrap him in my arms and take all his pain away.

"My god. He looks so…"

"I know," Harlan murmured beside me. "It's why I brought you here. Hannah has me, but James is so alone."

My heart tore clean in half at Harlan's words. I'd known James wouldn't have much support, but when Harlan had called, begging me to come to help James through this terrible time, I hadn't realised how bad things were. I could see it now all too clearly. James's pain, his loneliness, his fear. Everything he felt he wore for all the world to see.

But no one was looking.

"How could they ask this of him? That's his father."

Harlan and I stood at the top of the stairs in a small, out-of-the-way nook in Westminster Hall. We'd come directly here from the airport. James had another forty-three minutes to stand vigil over his father. He looked as though he'd barely make three.

"Has he been eating?" I asked.

"Hardly. He's not doing well, Presti."

That much was evident. But how did I help him?

"I don't... How do I help him, Harlan?"

"Being here is all he will need." Harlan's reply sounded far away, muffled as if spoken underwater. I realised then how hard this had been on Harlan too. A man who'd lost his parents so tragically, the memories this must be reviving.

"When Hannah isn't at the hospital sitting with George," Harlan continued. "I just sit with her. I'm just there for whatever she needs."

"Whatever she needs," I murmured. I could do that for James.

A never-ending stream of people filed along either side of Prince Arthur's coffin, eyes red-rimmed and wide. Some sniffled and dabbed away tears shed over a stranger, but James's eyes remained dry while people he'd never met mourned for his father. I did not know how James bore it.

Anger welled deep inside me that James couldn't mourn like

the rest of the nation. It felt wrong and despicable. And I knew there wasn't a damn thing I could do about it.

"Are you okay, Presti?" Harlan asked, his sad eyes watching me closely. I didn't know Harlan well, but I was enormously glad James had him in his life.

Never taking my gaze off James, I replied, "I can't stand seeing him like this."

"You care about him."

"I love him." The words fell easily from my lips.

"I'm glad." Harlan sighed wearily. How much rest had he had since the accident?

As I turned to ask him, movement caught my eye. James. Something seemed wrong. I felt it even if I hadn't seen how badly his legs shook now.

Without thought, I moved.

Racing down the stairs two at a time, I heard shouts and whistles as guards reacted to me racing toward Prince James. I didn't care. I had to reach James. Would they shoot to stop me?

Behind me, Harlan shouted, but his words sounded muffled. I didn't have enough in me to concentrate on anything more than James. Pushing my way through the line of mourners, I finally found myself at the bottom of the five steps leading up to the casket.

James stared down at me, with no recognition of who I was in his features. His eyes rolled up as his body went limp. I caught him awkwardly before he hit the ground. Balanced between two steps, I couldn't manage his more considerable bulk, and we sank together, me cradling his body with my own.

"James. James," I murmured, though I knew he was out

cold. Around us, chaos exploded. Guards tried to wrestle me from beneath James. Harlan's booming shouts tried to warn them off. But they didn't know who I was. They didn't realise James had collapsed. Mourners screamed, some ran, and others, no doubt, would have their phones out filming.

I wouldn't worry about anything but James. "He needs help," I screamed. "Get him a doctor."

All I cared about was the man lying askew on top of me. I desperately wanted him to open his eyes and tell me he was okay. But I was a realist — most of the time.

Trying my hardest to ignore the kerfuffle around me, I stroked James's face, whispering his name, willing him to wake.

Strong hands yanked on my arms and legs. I could only assume security personnel, fearing for the prince's safety, getting ready to rip me away from him. Didn't they know I'd gouge my own eyes out before I ever hurt James? Harlan continued yelling and remained ignored. Somebody else began shouting they were a doctor.

And then. Everything faded away.

Because James's stunning aqua eyes were locked on mine. This time with recognition. This time, he knew who I was.

"Presti?" he murmured.

"I'm here, James. I'm here."

"How?"

"Ah, a question for later. We're in something of a situation here."

Only then did James appear to register where he was and what had happened. Terror shaded the brilliant teal of his eyes; shame reddened his cheeks. And I hated it.

"Oh god," he moaned. "Oh god. What have I done?"

"You fainted, James. A perfectly human reaction to all the stress and grief," I soothed. James didn't seem placated at all. And then, I gently kissed his forehead because I am a fool who forgets anything else exists when I am in James's orbit.

His entire body tensed before I even caught up to what I'd done. "Oh, Jesus. James, I'm so sorry. Maybe nobody —"

"Ah, fuck it," James mumbled and kissed me hard and fast right on the lips.

The kiss didn't last long, and when James pulled back, he rested his forehead on mine, whispering, "I'm so glad you're here."

My heart felt so full that I feared it might burst. It galloped in my chest, beating wildly as James held me enthralled in his gaze. There might be a chance people around us missed the kiss, but I knew the princes 'vigil streamed live on YouTube, so... I suppose the entire world had seen or would see Prince James of England kiss another man in the coming hours.

Part of me felt apoplectic about my feelings for James being discovered, while another part didn't give a damn. James needed me, and I needed him. I needed him to be whole and happy, though I knew that to be impossible right now, given the recent events in his life. I might worry about this public spectacle in the coming hours and days, but at this moment, I had more important concerns.

"Perhaps we should get out of here," Harlan whispered, looking down at us with a hint of a smile and plenty of concern.

"I should finish —"

"James, nobody will think less of you if you leave here right now. You fainted." I kept my tone soothing, low, knowing James must be mortified that he'd collapsed so publicly and then, of course, the kiss that followed. He needed a doctor to check him over. But also, selfishly, I didn't think I could bear seeing him standing so still, so grief-stricken over his father's casket for a second longer.

"Um, I, ah, agree with your young man, Your Highness," a timid voice stuttered. "You should see a doctor, which I am. But I'm not your doctor. And I'm a paediatrician, though that doesn't matter. Your body works the same as a child's, just bigger, of course, but it works the same…mostly."

James and I stared up into the reddened face of a young woman who looked very much as though she were fervently hoping the earth would open its maw and swallow her whole right this second. She affected a kind of bob-curtsey as we continued staring, her gaze shifting nervously between mine and James's. I hadn't missed that she'd called me James's young man. I wondered if he'd caught it.

Unsurprisingly, James found his wits before the young doctor or me. "Thank you. You're very kind, and I shall be certain to see my doctor immediately." James reached for my hand, squeezing gently as he spoke.

He stood, pulling me to my feet with him. Had he hit his head when he collapsed? First, the kiss, and now he kept my hand in his warm one as he stood before god and everyone. "James? Are you sure you're okay?"

"Perfectly well, Presti. For the first time in a long time, I am perfectly well." He gently kissed the tip of my nose to punctuate his point.

Who am I to argue with his self-assessment? Smiling softly, I replied, "Very well. But I do think we should get you out of here, following the good doctor's orders."

"I agree," Harlan added.

As I turned to face Harlan, the rest of the room came into focus. Stunned faces surrounded us, a handful of grins but mostly utter confusion. Security had removed much of the public, but a handful still lingered, slowly making their way to the exits under the watchful eye of guards.

My talent for drawing attention seemed undiminished. Unfortunate, yet if it meant I got to keep James, I didn't care. "I don't care if everyone watches…us," I exclaimed. "Well, not all the time. I don't have an exhibitionist kink."

"Presti." James smiled. "I have missed you."

"Mm. And I you. I just meant…"

"I know what you meant." James shuffled on his feet, eyes downcast for a moment. "I hope you'll think the same a week from now when the press and public have torn your life apart."

"There's nothing for them to find. Except maybe that one time… Perhaps I'll tell you about that after we've been together for a while and you simply can't live without me."

James tipped his glorious head back and laughed, an action so incongruous given where we were, but seeing and hearing him laugh warmed my blood, making those pesky butterflies in my stomach flutter like crazy.

"This way, Your Highness," a burly guard interrupted. "We've cleared the back exit and have a car waiting."

"Will you come with me, Presti?"

"Astrid would murder me if I did not quote the great Gino

Vanelli here. So, 'wild horses could not drag me away from you', James."

"Oh boy," Harlan sighed beside me. I caught the last of his eye roll as I turned to him.

"People who are not deliriously in love simply do not understand the need to spout quotes from love songs at every opportunity, Har—"

Why had the air suddenly been sucked from the room? Why was James frozen mid-stride? I replayed the conversation in my mind.

Oh god.

Ohgodohgodohgod.

"James, I…"

"You love me?"

"Not quite how I wanted to express my feelings to you, but…yes?"

James smirked. "Are you asking me or telling me?"

"Telling. I do. Love you, that is. Very much."

Before James managed an answer, Harlan said, "I think we should get you two to that car."

"Quite right," James replied, the hint of a smile brightening the gloom.

At a slight nod from James, several of the burlier security guards closed in around us, guiding—almost manhandling—us out of the great hall where Prince Arthur lay in state.

The cool air blasted my face as we stepped out the door into the night. I hardly felt it. My senses, my awareness, had been entirely consumed by James. The warmth of his soft hand still holding mine, the hard press of his thigh along mine as we slid into the back of the car, the scent of butterscotch and citrus.

God, I loved him.

The relief in allowing myself to feel it and acknowledge my love for him felt overwhelming. I didn't know I could feel so…much. I didn't realise I could be so happy without bursting with it.

But I also knew it wasn't fair of me to feel such joy when James had so recently lost his father and may still lose his brother. His grief had to be my focus.

As the car purred to life and pulled away, James rested his head on my shoulder, a soft sigh escaping him. "I love you too, Presti."

He'd spoken the words so softly I had trouble hearing. Or maybe I found it hard to believe he felt the same way about me. This was a prince of England we were talking about. Prestidigitation Jones, a nobody from Kincumber, did not draw the attention of princes.

"I can almost hear you thinking, Presti," James murmured. "What is it?"

"Well. I was just thinking how utterly absurd it is that you could ever love me."

"Why?" James asked, sounding entirely perplexed. "You are kind, funny, sweet. You make me smile even when it feels as if the world is ending. Listening to you prattle on, as you once called it, about any subject soothes me. You are my home, Presti. My safe place. Plus, you are smoking hot."

"James," I scoffed.

He sat up, turned to me, and gripped my face gently in his hands. "Every word is true, Presti." James kissed my forehead, cheeks, the tip of my nose, and finally, my lips. "Every word," he breathed.

As we wound through the streets of London and James settled back into my arms, I thought that was enough. For now, this was enough.

Chapter Twenty-Two

FOR SOME ABSURD reason, I thought my father's death might soften my grandmother. I was wrong. As soon as we reached the palace, her yes-men were waiting for us, ready to pounce. At least Simon de-fucking-Montfort wasn't with them.

I should have known he'd be with the queen, creeping around her like a guard dog. Presti and I were ushered into her office; the disdain for us dripped from the yes-men like a living thing. If I had reached out to touch them, I would have felt their contempt. We'd broken the cardinal rule. Presti and I had shown the world our feelings for each other.

"James," my grandmother snapped. "What the bloody hell have you done?"

"Gran, I'm sorry—"

"Not bad enough that you fainted at your father's coffin, but then this total stranger comes to your aid, and you kiss him!

There, in front of everyone."

Simon stood behind my grandmother, a smug grin on his stupid face. I said, "He's not a stranger to me—"

"And at a time like this. When you are supposed to be grieving, showing respect for your father, not…engaging in foreplay with some person—"

"Just a minute!" Presti shouted. "I know you are the queen, and you've achieved the longest sceptredom of any monarch, and while that is all simply splendid, James is your grandson. Your *grandson*. And he has lost his father. He should never have been out there to begin with. Standing at his father's coffin while strangers parade past like some ghoulish spectacle.'

"Presti—"

"I've got this, James," he said and turned back to my grandmother. "I love James. I would do anything for him, but I will not stand by while you and that cockthroppled nitwit—" Presti pointed at Simon. "—try to make him feel bad for loving his father more than his duty. I won't allow you to make him feel guilty for having a very normal reaction to the trauma of losing his father." Presti looked around, glanced at me, and dropped into something between a bow and a courtesy. "Your Majesty."

To my surprise, my grandmother laughed. Simon de-fuck-ing-Montfort did not. He glowered at Presti, a flush raging on his face. "How dare you," he began. "You self-important little nobody. No one speaks to Her Majesty in that way—"

"Perhaps they should, Simon." I turned to my grandmother. "I love you, Gran, and I loved my father, but I'm not you. I cannot go out there and pretend I'm fine when really I'm falling apart. And I'm sorry the world found out about Presti the way they did, but I am proud to show them that this wonderful, perfect man loves me."

The room fell silent momentarily, and then Gran rose and stepped toward me. She looked tiny, almost frail, though I knew she had a strength most people never had. She reached up and patted my cheek. "You are right, James. Both of you are right. I should have put you first, not the public. Can you forgive me?"

"Of course." I kissed her cheek.

"Good. Then I think you should both go to your rooms, James, while Simon and I discuss how things will be managed moving forward."

"Thank you, Gran. I…"

"Hush now, James." My grandmother hugged me—an absolute rarity since I'd waded into the teen years. She felt small, somewhat fragile in my arms. Before this moment, I hadn't fully considered her immeasurable loss.

"I am so sorry for your loss, Gran," I murmured.

"And I yours." She kissed my cheek and gently pushed me toward the door. "Oh, and Presti, thank you. For being there for James when we weren't."

"You're welcome," Presti said, affecting another ungainly bow.

I took his hand and led him towards my rooms, chased by the scathing snap of my grandmother's displeased voice as she tore Simon a new one. I'd known my gran was in there, buried beneath the stern veneer of a queen. Presti's indignation at my treatment had broken through the royal crust straight into the heart of a granny.

"What is a cockthroppled nitwit?" I asked as my door came

into view.

"A fool with an overly large Adam's apple," Presti answered.

My bark of laughter echoed through the hall. "Christ, I love you."

Presti and I stayed hidden from the public for three days. We wrapped each other in our own small world while chaos swirled around us. Everybody, every single person, it felt like, had seen what happened between us at my father's casket. Rumours spun about us like a tempest.

We stayed silent, said nothing, and offered no comment. My grandmother kept away; my mother poked her head in, her eyes red-rimmed, and offered her support. Hannah stopped by and hugged me and told me she was so glad I had someone before her tears fell again, and she returned to George's side.

George… Well, he didn't die, but he didn't seem to heal either. He remained stuck in a coma.

Through this terrible time, I bore it as best as I could with Presti at my side. He stayed in my rooms and came to meetings about the upcoming funeral. We ate together and slept in each other's arms. I hadn't been brave enough to ask, but Presti told me he'd stay as long as I needed him.

In my head, that meant forever. I didn't tell him that though. But now that my great secret was out, I had no intention of letting Presti go again. What that meant and how our lives would look moving forward, I didn't know. I knew Presti had somehow become as necessary to me as breathing.

We didn't follow any media coverage about him, but I'd asked Scott, my private secretary, to keep an eye on it and keep me updated. I would not allow them to drag Presti through the mud to suit their agenda.

So far, Scott informed me that the worst they'd had to say about him was that he wasn't filled with noble blood. Back in Kincumber, Presti's friends and family had rallied the wagons; they said nothing to the press. Some fellow named Dominic had spoken to *The Sun* about an altercation between him and Presti years ago. Presti had bloodied his nose, and Dominic claimed it was for no reason. Only hours later, a second report came from Constable Dickens, who had been the officer involved. He'd made it quite clear Presti had a valid reason for hitting Dominic, alluding to something involving the treatment of animals.

In the end, Presti came out looking rather heroic.

Scott was already talking about getting Presti involved in animal welfare charities when the time was right.

But first, we had the funeral to get through.

Gran had finally relented to allow Presti into the church to sit with us. She might have shown her heart after the disaster at the princes 'vigil, but she was still the queen. Presti wouldn't be allowed — and he didn't want to — walk behind the coffin with me. He'd only met my father once, and neither of us thought his presence behind the cortege was a good idea.

Knowing he'd be waiting for me at the church was all I needed.

Mum had been fantastic, putting her foot down about Presti with Gran. I'd heard her scream that it was her husband's funeral, and she'd have at least some things the way she wanted. Despite my apologies for causing more drama at an already terrible time, Mum insisted that knowing I had someone who cared about me helped make things easier for her.

Truth or lie? I thought truth, especially after the few times I'd caught her watching Presti and me with the slightest grin.

"Have I thanked you for coming all this way to be with me?" I asked. Presti's head rested on my lap; my fingers slid through his curls, and he drew circles on my leg.

"Many times."

"Well, it bears repeating. Your life…" I couldn't articulate how his life would change after this; I didn't have the words. "It'll never be the same," I finished lamely.

"I know, James." Presti sighed, sat up, and took my hand in his. "But I don't care. I had a plan for my life. Goals. And I can still reach those goals. The path will just be a little different. You might think I'm giving up my privacy for you, James, but I know you are worth it."

Presti had said a variation of these sentiments several times over the last few days, yet I found it hard to believe it to be true. How could I be worth it?

"James? James, are you there?" Mum called now. Shouting in the palace was quite unlike her, and if she hadn't sounded so happy, I might have thought something terrible had happened — again. Presti and I stood.

"Here, Mum. What's happening?"

"It's George. He's awake." Mum barrelled into the room, collecting me in a furious hug. "He's awake and grumbling about being hungry."

"He's okay. He's okay if he's complaining about food." The happiness in my voice felt surreal, given my father's funeral was tomorrow. But my brother was okay. He was okay.

"Hannah said he's the same giant bellend he ever was." Mum kissed my cheek and squeezed me tight.

"Thank god," I whispered. "Oh, thank god."

"Wonderful news," Presti said with a smile on his perfect lips as he watched Mum and I dance about.

"Get over here, Presti," Mum sang, waving him toward us.

He came. He'd come because I knew he'd do anything for me. Mum dragged him into our arms, the three of us awkwardly hugging. None of us cared how we looked. We were too damn happy.

"Should we go to the hospital?" I asked.

"I've ordered the car. Are you both ready?" Mum asked.

"Should I—"

"Yes, you bloody well should," Mum cut Presti off before he could finish his thought. "You're in this family now, Presti."

Her words should terrify me. They should have horrified Presti, but instead, we turned to each other, sharing a smile.

"Okay. Well, yes, then let's go," he said.

Though still weakened by his ordeal, George looked better than I'd allowed myself to hope. Groggy from his medication, he still managed to take in Presti's presence and what it meant. He made a lame joke but smiled happily at us.

George hadn't yet been told about our father's death. Hannah and the medical staff managed to distract him from those thoughts until we arrived. Unlike me, who'd heard about it from Scott, Mum wanted to be the one to inform George.

Dad's death would affect George in a different way from me. Instead of being decades away, George's ascent to the throne would be only years, though sometimes I thought Gran might live forever.

At least George wanted this life. He'd rise to the occasion. He'd do his duty. And I would be there to help him. Knowing this didn't sadden me anymore; I didn't feel quite so overwhelmed by my life.

Because things had changed, the world knew about me, about Presti, and it hadn't stopped spinning. The world hadn't ended because I liked men—loved this man.

Before I could dwell on these thoughts, Mum entered the room after she consulted with George's doctors. She'd wanted to be sure he was strong enough to handle the news about Dad.

She made a beeline to George's side, her gaze catching mine as she passed. Her eyes shone with fear because of the terrible task ahead of her.

"What did the doctors say, Mum?" George asked.

"They said you are doing remarkably well, George," she replied, kissing the back of his hand.

"Well, of course. Was there any doubt? I am remarkable, after all."

My brother. Nothing wrong with his self-esteem.

Hannah offered a little groan, though the smile on her face at George's recovery couldn't be wiped away. Presti chuckled at my side, though his hand gripped mine tighter.

Thank god he was here. I didn't know how I'd get through this without him. Luckily, I didn't have to.

"George, honey," Mum began, "I'm afraid I have some awful news though."

George tried to sit a little higher, squirming as best he could with all the tubes and cords attached to his body. "What?"

"Do you remember much of the accident?"

"Nothing." George screwed his face up, his brows low over his eyes as he tried to recall the helicopter crash. "The last thing I remember — oh god. Dad. Dad was with me."

George's gaze flicked around the room, landing on each of us. Seeing the grief in each of us had to warn George of what was to come.

"He was, honey," Mum murmured. "And I'm afraid your father…didn't make it, George. His injuries…" Tears trickled down my mother's cheeks, her words trailing away, leaving George to fill in the rest.

"He's dead?" George asked in utter disbelief.

"Yes," I answered when the silence lingered too long. "I'm sorry, George, but Dad died at the scene."

George wilted under the weight of the news. Mum held one hand; Hannah held his other. I kept a hand on Mum's shoulder. George turned watery eyes to his wife. "I'm sorry, Hannah. I know this is much sooner — "

"George," Hannah whispered. "Don't you dare worry about me right now. I'm going to be okay… *We're* going to be okay. The only thing for you to focus on right now is getting better and mourning your father."

George wept. Quiet tears tracked over his cheeks as Hannah hugged him, careful of his injuries. Mum whispered soft words to him.

And me. I had Presti, who wrapped me up in his arms, rested his chin on my shoulder, and whispered that I'd be okay too and that he loved me.

We'd said those three words a lot over the last few days, but they never failed to take my breath away. Would they ever not surprise me?

Several hours later, we left to give my brother some rest. He'd been furiously sad at having to miss our father's funeral tomorrow. So distressed that Mum had called his doctors to see what could be done.

As a result, George would be there at the abbey, in a hospital bed with a doctor and two nurses in tow. The doctors refused to allow him to attend any other way, so George accepted, even though he hated the idea of the public seeing him so vulnerable.

He'd shed more tears when we talked about me and other family members walking behind Dad's coffin from the palace to the abbey. I told him I'd make him proud. He'd said he had no doubt of that, and then I'd cried.

Through it all, Presti stood at my side. A quiet sentinel, supporting me so ably in such terrible circumstances.

And the worst of it was I knew once the press got over the heir's death, they'd turn their full and nasty attention on Presti.

*

SWEAT POOLED AT the base of my spine as I walked behind my father's coffin on this unseasonably hot day. My legs were heavy, like they'd been filled with concrete. It felt as if I'd been walking for hours. Throngs of mourners lined the Mall, quiet with their heads bowed as we passed by.

Nobody cheered or waved flags, unlike so many other occasions I'd been here for. No one reached out to grab my hand. Though I felt their eyes on me, I believed these people grieved with me. Some of them might hate me after a respectable time had elapsed since my father's death, but today, I felt they were here to show their sorrow. I felt as if they cared about me. At least for today.

Presti had sent me away with a kiss this morning. The lingering feel of his lips on mine and the warmth of his strong body were the only things helping me put one foot in front of the other.

Fighting to keep tears at bay, I nonetheless allowed myself memories of my father. Moments we'd shared, both private and public, accompanied me on my long walk. Happy snippets of moments when we'd laughed together, lessons he'd taught me about being a royal, a man. The joy he'd found in the pages of his many books.

Though far from perfect, my father was a good man. He hadn't deserved to lose his life so young. His life had been full; he'd travelled so far and met so many, yet he'd still miss out on so much.

Grandchildren. So many birthdays and Christmases. My wedding.

He wouldn't be there to stand beside me during the coming storm of my outing. He wouldn't have the chance to get to know Presti, to see what an amazing man I'd chosen for myself.

I'd miss him terribly.

Soon enough, we reached the Abbey. The pallbearers did a magnificent job of carrying my father's coffin inside. I didn't think I was the only one holding my breath, praying they didn't drop it.

We marched solemnly down the aisle of the Abbey. Before I knew it, Presti's sweet face appeared. He gripped my hand as I moved to stand at his side. I wondered if the cameras caught it and then berated myself for thinking of something so inane at this time.

Off to the side and further back, George lay, slightly propped up in his bed. He should have been front row and centre, but at least he was there. I knew the service back to front, so I let my mind wander to more memories of my father.

He'd spent his life fulfilling his duty, and it had killed him. The crash was an accident, and accidents happen every single day. But, to me, all I could think was if we weren't royal, my father would never have been in that helicopter. What-ifs were useless though. My father had given his life to the crown.

As I thought about how he'd lost everything important because of his royal life, I became more determined I wouldn't do the same.

Chapter Twenty-Three

THE FUNERAL YESTERDAY had exhausted everyone. We'd all gone our separate ways upon returning to the palace. James and I hadn't seen a soul since.

After last night's meal, we'd slipped into bed, pulled the cover up, our noses almost touching, and shared soft-spoken thoughts until sleep dragged us under. Like all the other nights we'd slept together, some part of our bodies touched all night as if we were two magnets. I held James, and he held me. It didn't matter. All I knew was that we sought each other out even in sleep.

How would I bear saying goodbye? And I must say goodbye. Staying in the palace was a fairy tale, and I lived in the real world. No matter how much I loved James and he me, how could we ever be together?

Outside the windows, rain poured down on this grey

London day. At least there'd been gorgeous blue skies for Prince Arthur's funeral. Although grey clouds and heavy rain would have been more atmospheric, I wasn't sure James could have borne the added sadness.

As I lay there listening to the storm raging outside the palace, I pinched my thigh. I had to be dreaming. Right? Here I was in *the* Buckingham Palace, in bed, with Prince James of England snoring softly in my arms.

Yesterday, I'd sat behind the queen at the funeral for her son—the man who should one day have been king. I'd sat in on meetings with members of the royal family. None of this seemed real.

What did feel real? The pain radiating out of James's eyes every second. The palpable grief seeping out of his pores. The shock of his father's death seemed to be wearing off, the stunned expression of horror dissipating only to be replaced by forlorn acceptance. He still hurt. He would hurt forever.

The faint ring of my phone pulled my attention from the man in my arms. I slipped from James's bed—our bed—grabbed my phone, and walked into the bathroom.

"Astrid?"

"Why do you sound uncertain, Presti? Surely my name popped up on the screen," Astrid replied.

"It did, but I am a little bamboozled by life just now." I sat on the edge of the large bathtub. Ever since I'd seen it, I'd thought of little else but getting James in it. Soaking in a warm bath must be a revitalising experience. At least they always made it seem that way in movies and books.

"Quite bamboozled, I should think. How is James?"

I sighed heavily. The million-dollar question. "He's hurting. So much pain, As."

"I saw it. During the funeral. The only time he looked something like okay was when he saw you."

"You embellish."

"I do not. I am serious, Presti. James needs you now more than anything, I'd wager."

I sighed again and pinched the bridge of my nose. "I can't stay here forever."

"Whyever not?" I could hear the frustration in Astrid's voice.

"I have a life in Kincumber. Mum, Howard, my studies, you." Astrid's frustration seemed to be contagious.

"When you look back upon your life, Presti, will you be pleased with yourself for giving up a chance of love for me? Or your mother? Howard? Your studies?" Astrid paused, waiting for my reply. I said nothing.

"Presti, trust me when I say we will still be in your life, even if it's from ten thousand miles away. Everything you have here, you can have there."

"I think we're jumping the gun, as it were. It's too soon to be thinking about permanency. We're still… Well, I don't even know if I'd call what James and I are doing dating."

"All I'm saying is long-distance relationships with friends and family are far more manageable than with a lover."

"Very well, Astrid. I shall keep that in mind. But James hasn't even mentioned me staying. He hasn't even hinted at it—"

"Then let me fix that right now."

"James!" I shouted, jumping up and making an ungraceful

flurry of movement.

"Oh my," Astrid gasped through the phone. "Here comes the big declaration, and I shall be witness to it."

"You bloody well will not. I am hanging up."

"Oh, but Presti, think. You're on the verge of a morganatic—"

I pressed the button, ending the call with my dearest friend. I loved Astrid, but she didn't belong here at this moment with James.

James stood at the door to his bathroom, a hint of a smile on his lips, a look of bewilderment smudged with happiness in his soft blue eyes. His sleep pants were low on his hips, chest bare—the very image of perfection.

Yet, he said nothing.

For so long that I grew tense. Awkward.

Turning my back, I began running a bath, desperate for some distraction from the silence that had settled over us. As I worked, I babbled.

"This bubble bath smells amazing. Sandalwood. It's in all the romance books, yet I had no idea what it smelled like. I sniffed it when I was in the shower. Very nice. Manly. You know. And I hear baths are simply—"

"Presti?"

"Mm?"

"Stay with me," James whispered.

"Well, I did plan to share the bath with you, if that's okay—"

"Not for the bath." James stepped closer. I felt his warmth though my back was to him. "Not just for the bath. Stay with me, please. I want to see if we can make this work. I want to wake up with you and fall asleep with you. I want to watch you while you're sitting in my big armchair reading…whatever it is you were reading that brought that secret smile to your lips. I want to share my days with you. I want to tell you how the Prime Minister of Canada stutters when she's nervous and how the Foreign Minister of Ghana rubs his brow when he's lying. I want to hear about how King's holly can live up to 135,000 years and can clone itself or how tasty and nutritious the elephant yam flower is. I want you, Presti. All of you. I want us."

Well, damn.

"I know I'm asking a lot," James continued. "The press will be all over you—no more privacy. And the worst thing is I'm asking you to leave your home, your family. It's selfish and unfair, but I'm asking because I don't know how to be without you anymore. I don't *want* to be without you anymore."

"James," I whispered. I turned and pulled him into my arms. "I want all of that with you too. But is it too soon?"

James shook his head, his soft hair brushing against my cheek. "No buts. Maybe for some, it's too soon, but not for me, not for us. I've been waiting my whole life for you, Prestidigitation Jones. My whole life."

I kissed him then. How could I not?

We kissed for an age, soft, tender. Sometimes hard and more urgent.

We slid into the hot bath, the bubbles popping gently against our slippery skin. James sat between my thighs, his back against my chest. I held him and petted him.

"I'll stay," I whispered.

Chapter Twenty-Four

IT WAS TIME.

Jangled nerves pinched my insides as I watched everything being set up. My sitting room had been rearranged for better optics—whatever that meant—floral arrangements added, photographs purposefully placed on the table behind where we'd be sitting. Cameras loomed to catch every angle. Scott fluttered about reiterating what would and wouldn't be tolerated in the long list of questions we were to face.

Six weeks had passed since my father's funeral, and it was time for me—us—to address the world. To answer the questions printed every day. To silence the falsehoods. We'd chosen Marianne Drysdale as our interviewer. She was professional and well-liked, and Presti said he felt a good vibe from her.

He stood silently watching her now as last-minute make-up was applied, her hair fluffed and ready. I paid no attention to her.

As always, Presti commanded my attention. He wore a sapphire blue suit, a darker navy shirt, and no tie. His wild curls remained untamed, just as I liked them. His hands trembled, yet that confidence in who he was never wavered. Even when the hatred from some quarters spat at him, he refused to apologise for who he was.

In the quiet dark of the night, he told me how much he hated the fame he'd acquired since that day in Westminster Hall at my father's coffin. He also told me how worth it I was. A day never passed without him telling me he'd fight the world for me—for us. And a day never passed in which I didn't hold him in my arms and tell him the same.

Today, we'd be telling the world. We'd be sharing our story. Marianne would carefully guide us through how we'd met, what we meant to each other and what the future held for us. The topic of my sexuality would not be explicitly mentioned because…well, duh, people could guess. I'd insisted upon this. George never had to come out as straight to the world, so I didn't see why I had to come out as gay. The fact I was presenting Presti as my boyfriend was enough.

"Hey," Presti murmured as he gently squeezed my hand. "Are you still okay to do this?"

"Yes. Are you?"

After weeks of planning, meetings, and negotiations with my grandmother, dark smudges dusted the fragile skin beneath Presti's eyes. He'd been shocked and indignant about how much sway people like Simon de Montfort held over our lives. I'd never liked Simon, but Presti verged on hating the man.

"Certainly. I shall be breviloquent, but I intend to show the world how much I care for you, James Wales." Presti smiled and pressed a kiss to the tip of my nose.

He'd taken to calling me James Wales at certain times to remind me that he didn't see me as a prince. To him, I was the man he loved. I lifted our entwined hands and kissed his knuckles.

"Let's do this, then."

We sat on the couch, facing Marianne across from where she had taken the single armchair. She glanced up quickly and smiled before returning her attention to her notes.

Then the producer began counting down…

"We are joined tonight by His Royal Highness Prince James and Prestidigitation Jones, the young man who has been the subject of speculation for some weeks now. Welcome to you both," Marianne began.

"Thank you," we said simultaneously.

"You've both agreed to this interview tonight to end the speculation over your relationship. So, let's be clear, then, what is your relationship?"

It had been agreed that any questions not explicitly addressed to Presti would be answered first by me, and then Presti was free to add anything he chose. It had been Presti's idea, and I'd accepted it because I'd give him anything.

So, I answered, "Presti and I are in a loving, committed relationship and have been for some weeks, though we've known each other for far longer. If we have to label it, Presti is my boyfriend."

"And how did you two meet?"

We shared our story, each adding small bits to complete a whole picture. Not everything was shared, and it didn't need to be. We were public figures, but the public couldn't have all of us.

"So, you have moved to London now, Presti?" Marianne asked.

"In the process. I'm still at university and wish to complete my studies, so I'm organising to transfer to one of your fine tertiary institutions as soon as possible."

"And you're studying…?"

"Ethnobotany. It is a remarkable subject. And I'll leave it at that since once I get started on the topic, I can give quite a twarvlement."

Presti squeezed my hand and flicked his gaze to me. He'd been quite concerned about falling into using some of those unusual words he and Astrid loved. He told me he didn't want to come across as a word-grubber — one who uses obscure words in everyday conversation, he'd explained. I told him to be himself.

"Twarvlement?" Marianne asked, looking quite confused.

"Um." Presti shifted. "It's a long-winded speech. My dear friend Astrid and I often read books with copious lists of forgotten or obscure words. It was a bit of a game for us. Became something of a habit. Sorry."

Behind the cameras and crew, I heard Astrid murmuring frantically. I could only imagine she was delighted she'd been mentioned. She, Larry, Penelope, and Howard had been here for two weeks. And they'd brought a breath of fresh air to the palace halls.

Mum loved Penelope, and she'd helped my mother through the acute grief of my father's death. After their rocky start, George and Astrid got on like a house on fire. Secretly, I think George enjoyed Astrid standing up to him. It was a novelty.

"No need to apologise, Presti," Marianne said. "I love words.

Happy to know a few more. And would you tell us a little about Astrid and the rest of your family? Are they happy for you or sad that you'll be leaving?"

"Both, of course. Astrid has had Larry in her life for some time now, and my mother has Howard, so they all understand how it feels when a great love comes into your life."

"And is that what this is? Between you and Prince James? A great love?"

Presti leaned into me, turned, and caught my gaze with his. "The greatest," he answered.

Epilogue

ALMOST EIGHTEEN MONTHS had passed since I first set eyes on Presti, but I don't think he'd ever looked as beautiful as he did today with my brand new niece cradled in his arms, cooing and gurgling up at him. Hannah and George often sought Presti out when Grace couldn't be calmed. She always quieted in Presti's arms.

I watched him rocking gently, cooing back at her, his face alight with joy as he stared at her. Since my father's funeral and Presti's arrival on the world stage, he had amazed me every day with the gracious way he'd handled the intrusion of the press into his life.

Our life.

We were a unit—the two of us together against the world. We'd faced our share of hate and criticism, but most days, the venom flowed over us like water over rocks. We hardly felt it. We were stronger together.

"Have you done it yet?" Harlan asked as he came to stand at my side.

"No."

"What are you waiting for?"

"What if he says no?"

Harlan snorted. "I think that's unlikely."

Presti loved me. I knew that. But that didn't mean he'd want to marry me. Weeks ago, I had planned my proposal. A romantic, candlelight dinner. Slow dancing afterwards. Then, I'd take him onto the terrace under the stars, get down on one knee, and beg him to be my husband.

My nerves held me hostage though. How would I survive if he said no?

Grace's christening began in a few hours. Once we'd gotten through that, perhaps tonight would be the night. Presti had been to several royal engagements with me, and other than Hannah, I think he was the one people wanted to see most. For some, I think it was a morbid curiosity to see the man who'd turned their prince gay. Yep, that was a thing some people actually believed.

For others, he and I were inspirations. Some just loved love in all its forms and wanted to be a witness to it. Of course, Presti's beauty brought others to look at him—that one I understood. I could happily sit, stand, or lie and watch Presti for hours.

Though he was happy here, I knew he missed Australia. He missed his family. I intended to change that.

People who were part of my large, extended family filled the room now as we waited for the christening to begin. I knew them all, some better than others. Apart from Mum, George, Hannah, and Harlan, I only saw the others at royal events or occasions. I didn't spend hours on the phone or video calls with them as Presti did with Astrid and his mum.

Presti had sacrificed so much to be with me. It was past time I reciprocated. I'd already spoken to Gran and let her know I'd be stepping down as a senior royal. I'd told her if things went as I hoped, I'd be moving to Australia with Presti. She'd grizzled at first, but then — surprisingly — Simon de Montfort had come to my side. He'd talked Gran into appointing me as her representative in Oceania.

For a split second, I'd been shocked, until I realised Simon got what he wanted. Me gone. I didn't care because I got what I wanted too.

All I had left was to tell Presti and ask him to marry me.

Nothing much. Just placing my happiness in one little question.

I could do this. I could.

Look at what I'd done already. I had the most amazing man in the world in my life. He loved me. *Me*. Some days, I scarcely believed it. I mean, look at him.

Look at him.

Prestidigitation Jones was perfection. I watched him across the room pressing a kiss on my niece's forehead. I saw her smile at him, her tiny fist gripping his finger and watched his curls bounce as he laughed when she blew a raspberry. In a gilded room, Presti was the most golden thing in there.

I fucking adored him.

Look at him.

"Hey!" I shouted clear across the room. Everyone stilled —

shouting wasn't done in the palace. Presti looked over to me and smiled his beautiful smile.

"Marry me?"

A handful of gasps filled the air. Presti smiled wider and laughed. "Name the time and place, and I'll be there."

About the Author

Karrie lives in Queensland, Australia, where the scorching heat can sometimes be too much to handle. She's been blessed with two adult sons who embody kindness and compassion in all they do. No matter if she messes up everything else, she's proud to say those boys are her greatest success.

She's always been a storyteller, sometimes to hide from reality and other times just because she could. The sheer notion of others finding joy and solace in her tales continues to be a source of disbelief and immense gratitude.

Her everyday joys are her simple pleasures of reading, crafting stories, indulging in cups of tea, and relishing dark and stormy nights.

Despite having spent five decades on this mortal coil, she finds herself still waiting for that elusive feeling of being a true adult.

Email
karrieromanwrites@gmail.com

Website
www.karrieroman.com

Other NineStar books by this author

Until You Series
Shipped

Sentinel

Trusted

Valor

Standalone Titles
Saved

Advent Adventure

New Year's Shippin' Eve

Beyond Identity

Sons of Rome

CONNECT WITH NINESTAR PRESS

WEBSITE: NINESTARPRESS.COM

FACEBOOK: NINESTARPRESS

X: @NINESTARPRESS

INSTAGRAM: NINESTARPRESS

BLUESKY: NINESTARPRESS

THREADS: @NINESTARPRESS

www.ingramcontent.com/pod-product-compliance
Lightning Source LLC
Chambersburg PA
CBHW060250100726
47907CB00003B/836